Enigma 2

Kiminique Williams

Printed in the United States of America.
ISBN: 978-0-578-64542-1
First Printing, 2020
www.authoresskiminique.com
Shreveport, LA 71109

Dedication

IN HONOR AND REMEMBERANCE OF
PIECES OF MY HEART:

My MOTHER –
Sharon D. Robinson "Ro"

My BROTHER –
Felton B. Williams II "Troopa"

My GRANDMOTHERS –
Mamie G. McCrady Robinson "Granny" &
Mildred I. Mourning Williams "Mommee"

My GRANDFATHERS –
Sam Robinson "Grandpa Sam &
Tommie J. Williams "PawPaw"

My Great-Grandmother –
Clara Epps Montgomery

I thank God so much for each of these individuals
and the lives they lived. Most importantly, I thank
God for the gift of writing as it has been my outlet.

Enigma is defined as a person or thing that is mysterious, puzzling, or difficult to understand. Each character in this book brought forth enigma in his or her own way. This novel is based on fictional characters. Although, one or all may remind you of someone that you may know - including yourself.

Chapter 1
Tabitha

"Trenton Vermont, I have told you that I don't do drama. Yet, it has still presented itself to me. You, sir, are drama. For you to belong to someone and disrespect her repeatedly, I know that I don't want any dealings with you. After she threatened me the first time, I should have gotten a restraining order against you and her. Hell, I should have had her ass arrested because not only did she threaten me, but she threatened my boys as well. This is my last warning before I make legal moves," Tabitha said before she hung up.

As she was getting ready to go out and celebrate her new position with work friends, including Becca, she stood in the mirror and stared at herself. She was transitioning from being stationed to becoming a travel Nurse Practitioner. Getting out of the office setting and avoiding Dr. Vermont was mandatory for her progression, especially with all the drama that came along with him.

Becca called while Tabitha was getting dressed.

She answered, "Hey B, what's going on? Are you—"

"Bitch…I know we are about to go out, but I had to call you. Why the fuck have they been sucking and fucking in the ambulance bay? These folks do the muthafuckin' most." Becca cut her off as usual.

"Now, you know I don't want to hear that - especially not right now. Are you almost ready? I'm practically out the door. I will meet you there. Tell me about that place later not tonight - *later*." Tabitha stated.

"Trick, I know you didn't cut me off," Becca responded. "Whatever... I'm almost done anyway. Don't take your ass in there without me. I'll pick you up from your car so we can go in together 'cause I don't need you walking by yourself. I know you don't get out, so just calm down. I will see you in a bit."

It wasn't long before Becca pulled up to Tabitha's car and waited for her to get out so that they could find a closer parking space and walk inside the lounge together. As soon as Tabitha was seated in the car, Becca was already cussing about the way her clothes fit. She had already been drinking and was ready to drink some more.

She demanded, "Fix my bra, bitch. Unroll my shirt and snap this necklace while you're back there."

Tabitha adjusted Becca's clothing as instructed. A few turns and a park later, they were at the door. Becca was dancing before she even made it inside. Some of the ladies they were meeting were already there in the reserved section. They all took shots as soon as Tabitha and Becca arrived. The group downed a few more back to back between selfies, videos, and "usies." Everyone was dancing and enjoying the night.

As Tabitha danced along the wall in a zone of her own, her senses led her eyes to connect with eyes of a chocolate gentleman staring and smiling at her. She smiled back at him and continued to move to the beat. Just as the song was ending, she began to make her way to the restroom to freshen up. When she exited the bathroom, the guy was standing in the area near the bathroom talking on the phone.

As she passed him, he reached for her arm. However, he was still on the phone. His rudeness caused her demeanor to change as she snatched away and went to the bar. When she reached to pay for her drink, the same guy pushed her money away and offered to pay. Tabitha frowned and rejected his offer by paying for her own drink.

"Bartender, can I have whatever she's drinking and a Henn and coke?" the guy asked, insistent upon buying her at least one drink.

This time, she accepted his offer. She thanked him and headed back to party with her girls. The handsome stranger smiled and watched her make her way through the crowd with both drinks in her hands. She continued to dance, drink, and enjoy the night with her girls without even glancing back in his direction. After a few more songs, Tabitha noticed the time and gave the ladies the "time to go" look. They obliged as they danced their way out the door.

As they walked and recapped their night, Tabitha noticed that the guy from the bar was not far behind. He was trying to get her attention. She finally stopped with an attitude. The rudeness that she gave off rushed the guy to address her.

"Excuse me, again," he said, trying to catch his breath, "I would love to see you again, but I had to meet you first. I'm Dominick Sullivan. May I please ask who you are?"

Tabitha laughed and blushed before replying, "Hi Dominick. I'm Tabitha Morgan. I like your style, but I'm not who or what you're looking for. Weren't you just on the phone in the club? I'm not a hook up, baby."

"Let me find out myself if you're who or what I'm looking for. Give me a chance. I may be who you've been waiting for. Here's my number. Use it," Dominick said as he began to walk her to her car. He stopped before walking any further. "Do you mind if I walk you to your car? I'm not a stalker, and I'm not trying to hook up. Although we are both adults, we're too old for that."

Tabitha laughed as she agreed to allow him to walk her to her car. Before they could take another step, Becca interfered, yelling, "Look sir, I don't know you! I brought her here, so I will take her to her car."

"Go ahead with your friend, and we'll talk soon. Here's my number," Dominick said with a smile before handing her a business card and walking away.

Without another word, Tabitha walked back to Becca's car and got in. When they approached Tabitha's car, the ladies said their goodbyes. Becca pulled off when she saw that Tabitha was safe inside her car with the engine running. Instead of pulling off and heading home, Tabitha immediately called Dominick to come back and chat with her. Shocked to receive her call so soon, he quickly walked the few blocks back in her direction and met her at her car.

As Dominick approached her window, Tabitha let it down to talk to him. After a while, she exited her car to stand with him and continue their conversation. They talked for nearly an hour about everything from their families to social media. As much as they were enjoying the vibe they shared, it was getting late. So, they wrapped up their conversation as Dominick opened the door so that Tabitha could get in. Before he could close it completely, she stepped back out of the car and reached to shake his hand.

"Thanks for being such a gentleman. That's rare these days," she said, still holding his hand.

Dominick was intrigued by her politeness after the rough start they had. Before he could speak again, as if on cue, Urban Mystic's "In the Morning" began to play on the radio. Tabitha embraced Dominick, wrapped her arms around his neck, and danced with him to the song. Her hands slowly rubbed his neck seductively. She grazed her fingers along his face, touching his beard gently. She began to kiss him aggressively but passionately. Defenseless, he kissed her back as his hands began to travel across her body. In the heat of the moment, they began undressing each other while working their way into the backseat of Tabitha's car.

"Wait... Hold up. No... We can't. I can't. I can't... do this. I don't know you, and you don't know me. I apologize, but this cannot happen," Tabitha interrupted, breathing heavily.

Dominick didn't argue nor did he try to advance. He just readjusted himself and helped Tabitha out the backseat and into the driver's seat. Placing a kiss on her cheek, he removed his hat and said, "It's totally fine. We'll have time for that later when we get to know each other. I would much rather get to know you first. Call me when you make it home. You're okay to drive, right?"

Tabitha finally looked up from her embarrassment and saw that Dominick was bald underneath his cap. Her body warmed up in a way that it had never done before.

She stuttered, "Umm. Oh. Oh. Umm. Ok. I—I - I will—Umm. I'll call you when I make it home. Thank you so much and again, I apologize."

As she drove off, her legs began to shake drastically. Before she could to get onto the interstate, she called Dominick and asked him if he would stay on the phone with her until she made it home. They talked and asked the basic introductory questions. He was from out of town. It was his first time in Colston, and he was only there for business. He would only be there for another full day and a half. The two arranged a brunch date for hours later since Sunday was his departure date.

"Where are you staying while you're here?" Tabitha asked.

Dominick responded, "I'm staying at the Hilton not far from the bar. I walked down to the lounge to get out of that room. I'm sharing a room with my co-worker. That's who I was on the phone with at the club. I was trying to get him out to have some fun. We rode our tour bus down; no one drove personal vehicles."

"Oh ok. I hope those are facts. By the way, I've made it in the house. Thank you. I'm about to shower and get this smoke off me. Have you made it back to the room yet?" Tabitha asked.

"You're welcome. I'm in the hotel, but I haven't entered the room yet. I don't want to wake my roommate. But, go ahead and tidy up. I'll see you in a few hours. To clarify your hopes… Those were definitely facts. I don't have a reason to lie to you, Miss Lady." Dominick replied before hanging up.

Not even an hour after hanging up, his phone rang again. Tabitha was calling back.

Dominick answered, "Hey what's going on? Is something wrong?"

"No, there's nothing wrong. I just can't relax. I can't calm my body down at all. I'm not the type of woman that just sleeps with a person that I don't know, but my mind and body want you to a degree that I cannot explain with words. I can only express with demonstration. I've had time to think about it, and I'm sure that I want to go there right now. Come out to the lobby, please..." Tabitha said.

As Dominick stepped off the elevator, she stood there wearing a fitted silk gown. Immediately, they kissed and hopped back inside the elevator. The doors closed behind them quickly. Dominick pressed the button to the rooftop of the hotel. As they kissed, she made her way to his erection and strapped protection on him. Then, she lifted her leg and inserted his hard penis inside her. With her back pressed against the mirrors in the elevator and her legs wrapped around him, Dominick's first stroke released such a strong whimper of pleasure from her that they both reached their first climax before the elevator reached ninth floor.

By the time that they made it to the rooftop, the second session of intercourse was unfolding. They made their way to the rooftop's furniture. Dominick sat on the outdoor sofa while Tabitha rode him with her legs straddling his shoulders. He flipped her onto her back with her legs still over his shoulders. She was taking every inch of his chocolate penis. From slow strokes to straight pound actions, the two enjoyed every second of their decision to take it to that level as strangers.

At the tip of his climax, Dominick screamed out, "Woman! Tabitha! Shit!" while gripping her around the neck.

Tabitha, trying to control her orgasm, released such a massive puddle of juices that they both were wowed with laughter and relief.

Chapter 2

Allie

Allie was preparing a bottle for Devan when the doorbell rang. When she answered the door, it was the mail carrier delivering a certified envelope addressed to Devin Peterson.

"I'll sign for it. I'm his wife. He's not here right now," she said.

"Do you have any identification verifying your relationship to Mr. Peterson? I need to match the last names specifically for this document since the addressee is not present," explained the carrier.

Allie didn't hesitate to grab her driver's license, nor did she question the policy that was explained. She presented her driver's license and then signed for the certified mail. Once the transaction was completed, Allie called Devin and informed him about the envelope.

"Is it from the government? Is it a check? Is it a subpoena?" he asked, before stating, "I'm on my way. I'll just see when I get there."

Allie responded, "I'm placing it on the countertop so that you can see it when you walk into the kitchen. Devan and I are going to be in the nursery. Ava is in her room probably asleep by now. It's naptime."

Moments after they hung up, Devin was unlocking the door and walking in. Once he entered the house, he immediately opened the letter. The contents made him lose his balance. Suddenly, Allie heard a thump that caused her to run downstairs with the baby still in her arms. She found Devin on the floor with the letter still in his hand. Reaching for Allie, Devin crawled to her with face soaked with tears.

He began to apologize, "Babe, I'm so sorry. I should have known without a doubt that you wouldn't step out on me, but I had to make sure. You made me doubt not only myself, but you as well." Devin continued as he rub his son's arm, "I still had my thoughts and fears looking at and even holding Champ. I feared that he wouldn't be mine biologically, even with my name. Ava looks just like me. Her eyes, eyebrows, hands, feet, even her hair is like mine. She's undeniably my daughter. It looks as if I spit her out myself. Champ, I have questioned since before his birth. I prayed to God that he was mine, yet my mind wouldn't rest until this very moment with proof.

"The results from the test eased my curiosity. I can now look at him without finding faults of him not looking like me. I will accept that he kind of has my this or that but really looks more like you. I confess to you as your husband and your spiritual leader that I will forever be for you. This is a promise. This is one of the biggest tests of faith that I have ever had. I've held this in since that night I walked out on you and again the day that I requested the test. The sight of that man struck something in me that caused me to act out in such a way that embarrassment was not an important factor. I rebuked you, Allie."

Allie was standing there crying just as hard as Devin was, if not harder. As she cradled Champ and rocked him, she realized that he felt limp. He wasn't breathing the same. She stopped rocking and stared as she watched him struggle to breathe. She panicked as she dialed 9-1-1.

"Hello, this is Allison Peterson of 2770 Property Drive. My son isn't breathing properly. It's like he's gasping for air, trying to breathe. He's only ten weeks old. Please tell me what I can do until help arrives! I'm trying to stay calm, but I need to help him."

Devin jumped up and grabbed Champ. He held him in his hands and laid him sideways, while rubbing his back, praying, and apologizing to him. This was the first time Devin held Champ in a manner of acceptance and genuine happiness; although, he was in deep concern.

"Come on, Champ. Come on, Devan. Daddy loves you. Don't scare us like this. I'm so sorry, baby boy. You're going to be perfectly fine. I trust God fully. This is just a scare. Breathe, Devan. I didn't name you Champ for nothing. Overcome this thing. Breathe," Devin continued.

The paramedics arrived less than ten minutes after Allie hung up. They immediately checked Champ's oxygen to ensure that he was breathing properly without any blockages. They made sure his temperature hadn't elevated, and then they escorted them to the hospital where the doctor explained the baby's condition to Allie and Devin.

"I'm Dr. Nelson. What Devan experienced is infant sleep apnea. It's common for there to be instability in an infant's breathing. This is quite natural in the development of infants. In Devan's case with him being healthy, he may have experienced brief central apnea. Were you holding him during this episode?"

"Yes ma'am. Is it my fault, Dr. Nelson? Did I cause this?" Allie asked.

Dr. Nelson replied, "This is no one's fault, Mrs. Peterson, but we are going to keep him overnight for observation. Right now, he's doing wonderful. Nothing looks to be of concern, but because of his age and the reason he was rushed over, we must observe him and keep him hooked up to monitor his breathing and heart. If there are no further questions or concerns, I will leave you. Be sure to call or press the nurse's button if you think of anything."

Shortly after Dr. Nelson walked out, Tabitha with Logan and Drew, Becca, and Kami with Kaleb walked in.

"How is he doing," they asked collectively.

Allie just cried while Devin spoke to them about what was going on. He explained what the doctor had just told to them. Then, he took Ava and the boys to the hospital's playroom so Allie's friends could comfort her.

Chapter 3
The Catchup

Hugs were contagious throughout the room. The ladies began to catch up briefly. Then, Allie shared what had just taken place between Devin and the paternity test.

"He asked if I thought that Dewayne would be Devan's godfather along with Dawn and Montrell," she added.

Eyes of confusion followed by laughter filled the room just as Dawn waddled into the room. She was in tears at first but ended up in sync with the laughter before being informed of the reason behind it.

She responded, "He's probably afraid to say no or disagree with anything Pastor Peterson has to say. I'm surprised he didn't press charges against him. That's if he even remembers what happened that day."

They continued to laugh as they reenacted the day that Devin knocked Dewayne out. Their laughter awakened Champ, and he began to cry. Dawn washed up so that she could pick him up and bond with him.

"How's married life?" Kami asked Dawn as she comforted the baby.

Dawn smiled from ear to ear. "I feel like a queen. He treats me like royalty and makes sure everyone else does, too. He made sure that I was flown to you today, and we agreed that I'd just stay here until I have Lyric."

Jumps of excitement and hugs spread amongst them.

Becca chimed in, "I'm getting married." Showing off the ring that Jeremiah had given her, she continued, "Officially divorced and newly engaged. I want a small wedding, but we need you all there."

"We will definitely be there. I'm so excited for you. You have calmed down. You're not so edgy, and your mouth isn't so filthy anymore," Allie stated.

Tabitha laughed, "She hasn't been foul mouthed lately, huh?"

"Jeremiah doesn't curse much, and I noticed that it made him uncomfortable when I did," Becca explained.

Kami choked out, "So our comfort has never been a concern of yours?"

"All of you have known me since I began cursing. Therefore, had it been that much of an issue, someone would have addressed it. So, either it didn't bother you, or you became immune to it," Becca laughed.

Tabitha added, "Jeremiah is a good man. He's patient with you and exactly what you need in a man."

"What's new with you Tabitha?" Dawn asked with a concerned voice.

Tabitha hesitated. "Nothing new. Dodging Trenton Vermont. He's talking about leaving his wife - the crazy woman who sent the message that day. I'm not with that though. I agreed that we would be friends and *only* friends. This man is so crazy and so convinced that he's in love with me that he has mixed up his priorities. On another note, I met this guy though. He's quite different but much like my normal attraction. His name is Dominick. He's not from here, which is a bummer. However, it's workable since I travel now.

"Anyway, I was beating myself up about the fact that we had sex the same night that we met. Technically, it was the next day since it was after midnight, but you get it. Then, he was such a gentleman when I changed my mind. He was okay with us not having sex after I was the one who initiated it. That was before I literally drove back to get the much needed and worth the drive type of sex that we shared."

Everyone looked at Tabitha as she gave them details of the encounter with Dominick. They were in awe.

"Wow look at you! We are so proud of you. I'm speaking for all of us here. We — are — proud! You stepped outside of the box. Do we get to meet Mr. Dick-You-Down?" Becca asked proudly. "Wait, where did you meet Dominick, because you don't go anywhere, honey?"

Tabitha's face displayed awkwardness before she spoke to clarify. "The night that we were at the bar…"

"Oh shit, the chocolate man in the beanie," Kami cut her off, "with the beard and bowlegs. Girl! If I wasn't married, he could have gotten all in me on the first night, too."

"One hit wonder!" Becca yelled, startling the baby.

Dawn hushed them as she passed Champ to Allie. When she stood up, there was a wet spot in the chair where she was sitting. As she moved towards the bathroom, a gush of fluid hit the floor. Becca rushed to attend to her while Kami went to get a nurse.

Chapter 4
Dawn

"Oh no! It's too early. Call Montrell. No… wait. Let's not call yet. We need to find out what's going on first. Let me not panic," Dawn said while trying to calm herself.

The nurse immediately took her to the labor and delivery floor where she was admitted. Meanwhile, Kami called Montrell and then informed Dawn that he would arrive at the hospital in an hour.

Upon hearing that, Dawn began contracting. "Lyric is not trying to hear that!" she yelled.

Monitors were going off back to back as the delivery staff entered the room. It was time to deliver. Kami gowned up in the place of Montrell while the rest of the family was back and forth between Champ's room and Dawn's. Within fifteen minutes, Lyric made her debut into the world, weighing five pounds and three ounces.

By the time Montrell arrived, both Dawn and Lyric were sleeping. He stood and watched them in amazement as they slept. He approached Dawn and kissed her forehead. The kiss awakened her, and she introduced him to their daughter, Lyric Amour Carter. He picked her up and tears flowed from his eyes as he admired her beauty. While the couple got acquainted with their new bundle, the door opened. It was Toni. Dawn looked like she had seen a ghost.

She quickly broke the awkward silence and slowly said, "Toni, this is my husband Montrell. Montrell, this is Toni. I've mentioned her before. What are you doing here? I made sure that I was unlisted and private," Dawn asked Toni.

Toni smiled and replied, "Yeah, I know. I was passing by and saw your friends leaving out earlier. I remembered them from the last time you were here. Sorry to bring that up. I just wanted to see you and see how you were doing. Congratulations on both your baby and your husband. It's nice to see you doing so well."

Suddenly, a knock on the door brought in another familiar face. It was Blake. Before he looked inside the room, he was already talking.

"Toni, who are you visiting now?"

When he was completely inside the room, his face looked like a deer in headlights on a dark road. Toni abruptly began to shove him out the door.

While exiting she said, "It was nice to see you again. Glad I was able to meet you. Congratulations again."

By this time, Montrell had handed Lyric to Dawn and was headed to put the unwanted guests out of the room. His security had also made it to the room to escort Toni and Blake out and stand guard at the door.

"This is why I always travel with security. Now that we are one, so will you. The push of a button and voilà! They appear without warning. That's what they get paid for," Montrell explained to Dawn.

Without warning, Dawn's monitors began to beep simultaneously. Her blood pressure was up, and her heart rate was elevated. She and Montrell practiced breathing exercises until the medical staff entered. She began to calm down before the staff was able to help. After conducting a small overview exam to ensure that everything was fine, the staff exited the room. As they walked out, Mr. Clark eased around the door. Dawn's posture became more relaxed as she whispered, "Daddy!"

He washed his hands and hugged his daughter. Then, he shook Montrell's hand before hugging him tightly with joy.

"You have made me a happy man, Mr. Carter. First of all, you stood by my baby during a tough time in her life. Then, you asked for my blessing before asking my princess, my one and only daughter to marry you. You officially married her, and then the two of you give me a grand-princess. Now, you make sure I'm here to hold this princess by sending a personal car to pick me up and bring me this long way. Bless you, son. I love you."

Montrell helped Mr. Clark to a seat and laid Lyric in his arms.

He responded simply, "Thank you for allowing me the chance to make her my queen, Mr. Clark."

"Pop. Just call me Pop, but I'm definitely Lyric's Pop-Pop," said Mr. Clark as he kissed her small fingers. Once Dawn's vitals were at a safe level, the nurses advised her to rest.

Montrell whispered, "That's the last you'll ever have to see or hear from those two. May they have a happily ever after fucking up each other's lives. I only want the best for you, babe… the best for us."

Chapter 5
Becca

"I now pronounce you husband and wife. Jeremiah, you may kiss your beautiful wife Rebecca," Devin said as he married the two.

The guests and the wedding party smiled as they wiped tears from their faces. As if the moment was too perfect, all eyes quickly focused on the back door as a woman busted in yelling, "No! Wait!"

Becca immediately stopped kissing her husband and ran towards the familiar voice of the woman. Jeremiah tried to stop her, but before he could get to the door, she was already on top of the woman with her fists across her face. Blood was all over Becca's wedding dress as she repeatedly struck the woman. Suddenly, she stopped and walked off as if nothing had just occurred. Before she left, she whispered, "You brought this upon yourself Nicole. I asked you to stay away from us. Then, you disrespectfully showed up to *our* wedding."

Nicole was just lying there with her face swollen and bloody, laughing as Becca walked away. Tabitha ran to her and applied pressure and bandages, trying to clean her up.

"How did this woman get in here? Who let her in?" Tabitha asked as she looked around the room at no one in particular.

Everyone just looked around and feared to say anything in response to Tabitha's question. They all had looks of confusion on their faces as their eyes stared at the door that Nicole entered before disrupting the wedding. The sounds of sirens followed by the entrance of paramedics and police officers added to the excitement. A couple of paramedics escorted Nicole out on a stretcher and loaded her into one ambulance. Another group transported Becca whose ambulance was followed by police officers. They were both taken to the hospital. Nicole was examine and released while Becca was examined before going to jail.

As Becca sat in the cell with broken bones in her hands, she showed no emotion or remorse for her actions. In her mind, Nicole deserved every blow and more. She laid back, still wearing her wedding dress, closed her eyes and fell asleep. Moments later, she felt a nudge in her side that awakened her. When she opened her eyes, she was home in bed beside Jeremiah. She jumped up with confusion. *Was this a dream or was this real?* she thought to herself. However, instead of asking her man, she decided to just let the day play out.

"Babe, are you okay? Your breathing changed while you were sleeping," Jeremiah said.

Becca took a deep breath. "Thank God; it was just a dream!"

As she calmed her heavy breathing, she glanced at her dress bag hanging on the closet door and took another deep breath. She turned on her side, stared at Jeremiah, and gently kissed his lips. His look showed that he knew just how to enjoy the gentle side of Becca because it was rare that she displayed it. He grabbed her and pulled her closer. He held her with security before planting a sensual kiss on her neck. She began to kiss his chest with gentle pecks.

Her kisses moved from one nipple to the other as she eventually gave tongue teasers. She worked her way downwards, licking abs to navel through his forest until she reached the limb that was far stretched. She went into satisfactory pleasure-giving, determined to blow his mind. Smiling at his erection, she knew just how many licks it took to get to the center of his tootsie pop. With a few oral motions, Jeremiah groaned and unfolded with jerks of release.

"How the fuck do you do that?" he asked between breaths.

Becca laughed and seductively gazed into his eyes as she got up and headed towards the bathroom.

"Bae, did you file the restraining order against that bitch Nicole?"

Boggled, Jeremiah responded, "What? Nicole? Yes, I took care of that a long time ago. Where did that come from? Why is she coming back up?"

"I keep dreaming of her interrupting our happily ever after. This time if I didn't kill her, I damn near did while still wearing my wedding dress," Becca explained as she giggled.

Jeremiah stared at her through the steamy shower door before approaching her. He eased behind her and helped her finish washing up while kissing her body from top to bottom. As he slowly inched into her moistened jewel, he folded her downward to present the perfect arch. Then, he repeatedly stroked her until her leg was no longer shaking. After tapping on her ass and ejecting himself, Jeremiah reminded her of his feelings.

"I love you and want only you. We will be happy together in our forever after without any interruption from anyone."

Chapter 6
Kami

"Ma'am your card declined," the cashier stated as she passed the card back to Kami.

Kami's face changed instantly, and so did her tone.

"Declined?"

She took out another card and handed it to the cashier.

"Here; I'm not sure why it would decline. We've the funds."

The machine made the same declining noise as it did with the other card.

"I apologize, ma'am. This card isn't working either."

The cashier handed the card back.

"We can't try any other card after

two declined transactions. Can you pay with cash?"

Kami reached into her purse and went into the bottom where she kept money stashed if moments like this ever happened. She handed the cashier $920 to pay for the transaction.

"Thank you, ma'am. I apologize for the inconvenience. Let me contact my bank and credit card company to see what's going on. I appreciate your patience. I'm so embarrassed," Kami stated uncomfortably.

Immediately she dialed the bank's customer service number.

"Ma'am, your cards have been temporarily locked by the owner Jackson Reynolds," the representative informed Kami.

Kami snapped, "I'm Jackson's wife! My name is also on this account. How could he possibly lock my card without contacting me?"

She hung up without getting a valid response from the representative and immediately called her husband. Her phone call went straight to voicemail. Anger grew within her as she refused to call back or monitor her phone to see if he would call right back. Instead, she hung up and called Dawn who answered the phone breathing heavily.

"Hey, Boo. What's going on?"

"Dawn, is this a bad time?" Kami asked confusingly.

She replied, "No, I was just putting Lyric down for her nap. I had to run to silence the phone so it wouldn't wake her because I wasn't wearing my Bluetooth. What's going on with you? Is everything okay?"

"Hell no. Why did Jackson lock my credit and bank cards? I was just at VonRay's shopping, and my card declined. So, I called to find out why, and he has it locked. Luckily, I keep a stash tucked away in my purse for hard times. Jackson has been different lately. He's been coming home late every night for months now. I've noticed but didn't want to say anything because there used to be times when he couldn't come home at all due to work. Then, today I called him, and my call went straight to voicemail. That's a guaranteed first," Kami vented.

The phone beeped as Kami was talking. It was Jackson calling her back.

Dawn asked, "Do you need to get that?"

"I most certainly do. I will talk to you later."

Kami clicked over.

"Jackson Reynolds? What is going on?"

Jackson answered, "Kami, now is not a good time to discuss this. I had to call you back, but I still cannot talk right now. We will talk when I return home."

"Home? When is that Jackson? When will that be? When will you be returning home? When should I expect you?" Kami continued to ask questions.

Jackson talked fast. "Later, babe." "I have to go," he rushed as he hung up the phone.

Kami had just walked into the house from her embarrassing shopping trip. She went straight to their room and laid down across the bed. As soon as her body touched the bed, it registered that the house was not as clean as usual. She yelled for the housekeeper. After there was no answer, Kami dialed her number. During the conversation, she learned that the housekeeper had been laid off. Rather than make a fuss, Kami immediately began to clean up.

She straightened up the upstairs area and then worked her way downstairs. As she was hanging up her jacket in the coat closet, she stumbled across a black briefcase. After a brief moment of hesitation, she opened the briefcase and her jaws dropped in disbelief of what was before her eyes. There were pictures of Malik and herself at the shopping center, in a café, leaving the Four Points, and recently downtown.

She also saw paperwork with signatures from Jackson and Lauren, Malik's late wife. Kami dropped to the floor in shock, mortification, and betrayal. Her mind was in a million places. She was completely caught up with absolutely no escape. She questioned Jackson in his absence. How could he have known all this time and never said anything? Jackson had a complete case against her. Her questions brought forth fear. She remained in the same spot for over an hour before packing the information back into the briefcase like she found them and placing it back on the shelf.

An idea surfaced as Kami gathered her thoughts. She decided to take actions to make sure she had somewhere to go. However, before she could get all the way upstairs, Jackson was walking through the front door. He called her name and demanded that she come to him. Hearing the calm anger in his voice turned down her attitude, and she calmly walked downstairs. Before could get a word in, Jackson made her sit down and listen to him. She took a seat on the couch as he walked towards the closet where she had just returned the briefcase. Kami took a deep breath, hoping he wouldn't notice that she had been snooping. He placed the briefcase on the table and pulled out the evidence to show her.

He explained, "For two years, I have known about Malik Burns. His wife, Lauren, hired me after purchasing equipment from us before she passed away. She wanted a divorce because she knew that he was cheating but needed proof. After a quick investigation, I found out that her husband was cheating with my wife. My wife was the mistress that poor woman was concerned about. Her husband was calling you. Not only were the two of you talking and texting, but you repeatedly had sex. I just knew that you were smarter than you have shown me. You know my profession. So, surely you knew I would find out.

"Then, I confronted you and you lied to me. I had proof long before I asked you, and you still chose to lie to me. After this woman lost her life giving birth to the man's child, the two of you continued your affair. How heartless is that, Kami? That's scandalous. What did either one of us do to you to deserve what the two of you put us through? I could not tell her that you were my wife… Not immediately, but I had to eventually. We went through the records, and my name popped up because your phone is in my name. You made me look bad in front of my client. How would you feel if I told you that was my daughter that she died giving birth to?"

Jackson left Kami with that thought and walked away.

Chapter 7
Tabitha

Forgive me Father
For being the reason
Two are dwelling on parting ways
Parted from your ways
Now from one another
Asunder I have meant not to
Place them
I tried to be the glue
To bind them together
As they were drifted
Upon my arrival
Yet I failed to restore
Even with attempts
Created to be as I am
I meant only to revive them

Tabitha journaled her thoughts as she sat near her window. Just as she closed her notebook, her phone rang. It was Trenton Vermont calling.

"Hello, Dr. Vermont. What do I owe this call?" Tabitha asked dryly with sarcasm.

"Call me Trenton not Dr. Vermont. Please don't do me this way. I'm in love with you. You truly have a hold on me. I know what you said, but I cannot only be your friend, Tabitha. You deserve more than a friend."

"Yes, I do. But, you're a married man, Trenton, and I'm a single woman. I apologize if I made you feel that way, but the feeling is not mutual. I think you're an incredible, caring friend. Besides, I met someone. I really like him, and we have a positive vibe between us. I won't jeopardize my peace because you want to build a relationship with me outside of our friendship or acquaintanceship.

"Your wife contacted me and threatened me, and I fell back - so far back that I stop calling and texting you. Lines have been crossed and there is no fairness in any of this. Do us all a favor and make it right with your wife. That way, she doesn't bother me, and no one gets hurt physically, emotionally, or mentally," Tabitha explained.

Trenton begged, "Let me show you that we'd be good together. She knows that I'm in love with you. She sees that, and she fears you. You have a hold on me that's unexplainable. We've never had sex, so you know that it isn't sexual. Although, I'm sure that it's incredible. Choose me, like I have chosen you."

While Trenton continued to profess his love for Tabitha, a message from Dominick came to her phone.

"Hey Beautiful… I can't wait to see you again. I enjoyed your company. You're hilarious as well as beautiful… Oh, I've already stated that. Well, you're very beautiful. You're attractive from head to toe, and you're intellectual. I was thinking about you, so I shot you a text. Get at me when you can…

- Nick

That text made Tabitha forget that she was still on the phone with Trenton. She sighed in puppy love as she smiled at the screen. Her voice had lightened to a more pleasant tone.

"Nick… I mean… Trenton…I have to go. I will talk to you later. Sorry, there's nothing that I can do," Tabitha stated.

"Who is Nick? That's who has your attention, huh?"

"Bye, Trenton. I have to go." Tabitha hung up.

Chapter 8
Allie

Allie didn't sleep a wink when they returned home after Champ's release. She wouldn't take her eyes off him, while Devin never took his eyes off her. He looked at her in admiration as he found himself falling in love all over again. As she stood over Champ's crib, Devin stared from the door. Without saying a word, he walked in as she sat down in the rocker. He eased before her and began caressing her face. He applied kisses to her lips, and then moved down to her neck. He slipped off her panties, kissed her ankles, and ran his tongue up to her *sweetness*. Allie pushed him away in rejection as he rubbed her juices onto his lips with his tongue.

"This is not the right time for this, Devin."

As he scooped her out of the chair and carried her to the bed, she panicked.

"Take me to my baby! I need to keep an eye on him. I can't let him out of my sight!" she screamed, killing the entire mood.

Ava ran out of her room yelling and crying, "Mommy!"

Devin escorted their daughter back to her room and his wife back into the room with Champ. She stayed glued to their son's bedside for hours. When Devin decided to come back to the room, Ava was at his side with sadness in her face and questions rolling off her tongue.

"Mommy, when are we going to play tea party or dress up again? Champ is better now. Can I be your baby again? Can we play? Can we dance? Can we go see 'Secret Life of

Pets?' How about ice cream; can we go for ice cream, Mommy?"

Allie waved for Ava to come closer so that she could sit with her and Champ. The closer Ava got the tighter Allie's grip became with Champ. She hugged Ava but never laid her son down nor did she adjust him to make Ava feel special. Their daughter could sense the distance, so she slipped out of the hug and ran back to Devin.

Devin's position and facial expression changed as he forcefully stated, "Allie, the doctors sent him home with the Owlet to monitor his heart rate and oxygen levels. We can see it from our room or any room for that matter. We have cameras in here that are connected to our phones so that we can see both of our children with a touch of a button. Lay Devan down and go show our princess that she still matters. There is no reason under the sun that she should feel like she's not important. Allie, you made her feel that way moments ago. You couldn't even give her five minutes of your time."

Allie got up from the rocker, placed Champ in his crib, and went into the room with Ava. She and Ava spent the rest of the day together as she buttered her up with adventures and outings of her choice. Their day was filled with a trip to the nail shop, ice cream parlor, build-a-bear, and shopping. When they returned, Allie was greeted with boxes of books. She had completely forgotten about her book signing scheduled for the next day. She wrapped up her evening with Ava and immediately got on the phone to finalize the plans for the event.

The Next Day

It was book signing day and the line was out of the door. The turnout was beyond expectations, and Allie was in a great mood. Cameras were flashing as she took pictures with everyone who purchased a book. She signed countless books and had numerous small conversations with buyers. Suddenly, a familiar voice caught her attention.

"Well, congratulations, Allie Cat. You can make it out to…"

Before he could finish, she exclaimed, "Alfie! Or do strictly go by Topo Montego?"

"Montego will be fine. No one called me Alfie but you and your crew. Thank you, Allie Cat. I'm proud of you. This is my daughter, Ahji. She loves to write, too."

"Hello, Mrs. Allie," Ahji spoke with a strong accent.

Allie hugged her and then told Alfie, "You used to call me that when we first met."

He simply smiled with no words. The line was still growing, so Allie exchanged numbers with Topo and promised to call later. They were classmates from middle school through high school. He was from Nigeria and had a crush on Allie but respected their friendship enough to never openly tell her. Becca had given him the nickname Alfie from the TV show Alf because of how close his eyes were and how wide his nostrils were open.

Allie crushed back but was afraid to let him know because of how Becca talked about him. Topo was always a gentleman and smarter than most males his age back then. He went back home to Nigeria right before their high school graduation, so they had lost all contact with one another. This was her first time seeing him in years.

During the book signing, Allie had connected and reconnected with many individuals. That made her appreciate the way Devin spoke to her last night. Her parents also came to support her. Seeing them sparked a memory of her father telling her the role of a husband. Specifically, she remembered him saying, "If you can't follow your husband as a leader, then back off and trust him. Sometimes women get in the way by overtalking and trying to be the boss. You can be the brains behind the operation, but let the man put the plan into action. Let him be your muscle." Her mother simply added, "Don't be another bill; be the co-pilot. Let him lead. Just be sure to back him up."

Amid the thought and memory clutter, a customer asked, "What made you name this book *Missionary Euphoria*?"

Allie's response was, "Once you read it, you'll completely understand. I don't want to spoil it for you. When you do, leave me feedback. I placed a card inside your book with contact info on it."

As the last customer exited the store, Allie decided to try something different. She enticed Devin to assist her with a wardrobe change. He agreed and walked into the family bathroom behind her. After closing the door, she dropped his pants. His jaws also dropped once Allie swallowed his dick. At some point, she had eased minty candy into her mouth. She gave him the cooling sensation of oral sex before wetting his dick with spit during her deep throat technique that she learned from the grapefruit lady. Then, she slurped the orgasm right out of him and caused him to release loudly.

Moments later, a knock at the door caused Allie to peek out and whisper, "Almost done," to the manager as she stood by the door informing them that it was closing time. They got dressed and quickly packed up everything and took it to the car. Before they could pull off, Devin and Allie were at it again like teenagers. He booted her over the armrest from the backseat, eased his thumb inside her ass while his dick entered her love spot. He grabbed a fist full of hair and picked up where they'd left off.

He was pounding away, stroking like a dog in heat. He tried slowing down to postpone his nutt, but he was unable to resist the release upon her back. So, he went ahead and flipped her on top. Thankfully, they had taken the kids' car seats out of the back seat because the way she straddled and rode him had him mesmerized. The second nutt shot out like a virgin.

It was the first time in a long time that they engaged intimately since before Champ was born. Devin was in awe. He was ecstatic about what he had just received. The two were like bunnies for the rest of the night. Thankfully, Allie's parents kept the kids overnight.

The next morning Allie realized that she still hadn't checked her phone, even after picking up the kids. When she finally did, she had many missed calls, texts, and emails. As she went through the texts first, she replied per priority. Most of the messages came after the missed calls. This made the need to return some calls unnecessary.

Immediately upon receipt of Topo's message, she felt guilty because of the feeling that consumed her. She just felt some type of way about him. Still, after the last issue with Dewayne, she didn't want to cause any more trouble in her marriage, especially when it had just gotten back on good terms. However, she didn't want to ignore the message, so she replied:

Topo, how nice it was to see you after all these years. In the next few weeks, if you're still available to catch up, my husband and I would be glad to sit and chat with you. Until next time…

- Allie

Chapter 9
Kami

As soon as the last box was unpacked, there was a knock on the door. A sheriff was standing there readily handing Kami an envelope as he stated, "Kami Reynolds, you have been served to appear in court on the date in red. Sign here to acknowledge your receipt of this envelope and have a great rest of your day."

"Served?" Kami was confused as she looked at Dawn.

She opened the envelope and began to read further. Jackson had filed for divorce. Kami's body fell to the floor in disbelief.

"He said he didn't want a divorce. He said that he wanted to separate and give us time. He didn't waste any time either. Now, I'm faced with this pregnancy alone."

Dawn froze, "Pregnancy?"

"Yes, I didn't want to tell anyone about it because I wasn't sure if I was keeping it. I sure didn't want him to think that was my way of making him stay or forcing us to be together. I'm not going to keep it. I have enough going on," Kami confessed.

As soon as she said that, multiple messages came simultaneously to her phone. They were from Tyson.

Kami, I think Grace and I should have Kaleb until you get yourself together. He won't be alone, and you can still see him as much as you'd like. I know this isn't coming at a fantastic time... probably not a good time at all, but I wanted to ask before taking any legal actions by including "the folks" in our lives.

Maybe you didn't think about how this affects Kaleb, but he needs more time with his father, Kami. I'm not his babysitter. Damn. You have him to where everything is at his fingertips. He's a boy and should act as one.

Anyway, I'm asking you to let me help you until you get yourself back together. I'm not in your business. Just trying to help you while you get back to business.

-Tyson

Kami read Tyson's messages and threw her phone in rage. Luckily, it landed on the carpet and didn't shatter. She paced through the house, walking around the clutter from the move. Everything was unpacked, but some things had not been put away. As she paced the floor, she decided to call Tyson and address the issue. Her call went straight to voicemail, so she hung up and dialed Grace's number. Grace answered in her normal tone, and calmness overcame Kami immediately.

"Hey there, Grace. Is Tyson anywhere near you? If not, let me know when the both of you are available to sit down and discuss Kaleb. I received his text, and I didn't call to argue or disagree. I think that we should sit down and arrange appropriate living situations for Kaleb. I agree that we should do what is the most beneficial for him. I'm sure the two of you have had a conversation regarding this, and I just want the best for my baby. I'm going through a lot, and I don't want it to negatively affect Kaleb," Kami explained.

Grace's response broke Kami down. "Kaleb told us that you were moving into a new house - just you and him. He also said that he has watched you cry a lot. I watched Kaleb cry, and it tore me apart. He knew something was going on. He just didn't know what. You know children sense things even when we attempt to hide them. I feel partly responsible for your anger, but I had to talk to Tyson about it. So if you're upset about his suggestion, I accept the anger openly with no regret. No disrespect, but we are all Kaleb's parents. We want the best for him, and we are here for you as well because he needs you."

Still holding the phone, Kami was silent. Every word that Grace had spoken made sense and showed her the genuine love that she had for Tyson and Kaleb. Kami had to get a grip and make decisions sooner than later. She started by removing herself from the hole that she dug herself into by accepting her fuck up and moving forward.

Chapter 10
Small Talk with
Tabitha and Rebecca

Becca laughed, "You know I have to catch you up on work shit. I know you don't work there anymore, and I know you don't gossip. But, bitch, everybody fucking every muthafuckin' body. We know after the shit with Mrs. Vermont, talk started coming from everywhere. Questions were coming to me from bitches who never opened their mouths to even speak."

"See that's why I didn't want to even talk to the damn man from the start. I cold-shouldered his ass from the beginning, but this generous heart had hope and had situational perceptions. So, I tried to keep it friendly. I tried to meet the wife several times so that it didn't seem or appear as anything more. The one time that they were both free, I was not. So, I had to decline. I didn't allow anything sexual or physical to occur between us still to this day.

"Hell, I felt bad the day the car wouldn't start and that I allowed the man to help me. Well, that was until I found out that she was the reason my damn car didn't start in the first place. I operated in innocence, even during my vulnerability stage of asking him to be my date. I called and cancelled after openly telling y'all. This man had really clung to me, and it had gotten to the point of being uncomfortable. I tried to be cordial, but enough was enough. I had to avoid him and cut him off. I tried to do this maturely, but he wasn't having it. He continued to call and text, pleading for me to let him into my life," Tabitha explained.

Becca snapped, "It's okay. Forget about him though, boo. Jeremiah has a friend that he wants to introduce you to before the wedding. Don't be mad; you may like him. I just remember you asking me if he had a brother, so I asked him. The guy sounds good from what Jay explained. I haven't met him yet, but he sounds like your type. He's tall, bald, and dark-skinned. Oh, and he's single. He does have children with only one baby mama."

"I don't know about that—" Tabitha began but was cut off as usual.

"Damn, bitch. Be open. You're welcome. You may like him."

Chapter 11
Becca

"We're a week away from our 'I Dos.' How are you feeling about it, Jay?" Becca asked.

Jeremiah's reply was dry as he said, "I'm just ready to get the show on the road."

"Is something bothering you? Do we need to postpone?" Becca inquired.

Jeremiah's response took Becca by surprise. "Don't do that. Don't turn my words for your comfort. I said what I said and meant it exactly how it came out. Getting married to you is a dream come true. But the wedding is a show, and I'm ready to get that part over with. Rebecca, I would marry you anywhere because I love you. It's not for show or for 'cool' points. If it were up to me, we would already be married. That's how I really feel."

"Jay, baby, I'm sorry. I'm ready to be Mrs. Davis. I even apologize for not already being your Mrs.," Becca said apologetically shocked.

Jeremiah further explained, "Don't allow anyone or anything to distract you or worry you regarding this wedding. As long as your 'I do' matches mine, we'll be fine. We've worked through so much already, and there will be plenty more with marriage. This is not your first rodeo, but it's not the same bull either. Circumstances are different. We've established new love - different for both of us. That's why we can take this step and not second-guess our decision."

Changing the subject, he informed her that he wouldn't be home later tonight. If he did make it home, it wouldn't be at a reasonable time. His bachelor party and her bachelorette party were both that night. Everyone was excited about Becca's bachelorette party. She had no idea of how much fun would happen. So much was planned and so many unexpected guests were invited to help celebrate.

Kami had booked some dancers from Atlanta, Houston, and Chicago. Dawn had gotten an old firehouse as the venue. It had the pole and everything still in it. The decorations were unbelievable and spontaneous, and there was a "NO PHONES OR PHOTOS" rule. There would be male servers walking around wearing almost nothing. Becca's crew had planned for it to be the best fucking bachelorette party ever. In the car on the way to the party, Becca was blindfolded with no idea of what to expect. As her door opened, a hand reached to grab hers, but she snatched away once the two hands touched.

"Wait a damn minute!" Becca snapped.

Tabitha yelled from the walkway, "Trust the process! It's hired help! Grab the hand, and don't mess up the plan."

Becca allowed the hand to pull her from the car and lead her to the door. Upon arriving at the door, she was crowned and sashed. The music was banging, but the cheering within was louder. The blindfold was removed from her eyes, and she bucked them at the sight before her. It looked like an underworld sex escape. Neon lights were everywhere. It was foggy but clear enough to see without chaos. Before her was a server kneeling with a tray of drink options. Once she chose her poison, he handed her a shot glass already filled.

The ladies were ready to begin the night. With glasses in the air, the first toast was in honor of the bride-to-be. Right after, she visited the tables where vendors stood with necessary products for the occasion. Kerri sold her products from *Intimately Desired* including the Satisfier Penguin Pro, Orange County Cutie, and Sensualle Home Pro. The top products sold out before the night was over. Keyuna sold products to keep the yoni clean, including the Yoni Goddess wash, Yoni soap bar, and Yoni pearls. There were presentations that wowed and had the women intrigued - even more than the Grapefruit Lady's dick sucking show.

The place was filled with laughter, dancing, food, and music when a familiar face suddenly approached Becca. Tabitha stood smiling as she watched her recognize who the woman was.

"Chelsey?" Becca asked with uncertainty.

"Yes, bitch, it's me. Congratulations," she responded as they hugged and rocked.

Tabitha walked up just as the hug was over. "Surprise!"

The three took another shot for old times. As different faces from the present and past took shots to celebrate, Becca was relaxed just in time for the entertainment. The way the seating was arranged, Becca was seated on the raised area near the pole. As the music changed, the first dick was sliding down the pole. His name was "Poison." This chocolate dream come true was dressed as a firefighter, and the hose he was carrying was "heavy." He tied his suspenders around Becca's hands as he placed them over his head before picking her up and working her out.

Poison was down to bare skin and

boots as he bent Becca over and made her touch her toes with her hands still tied. As the first line of entertainment, he set the bar high. To add to the fire, he lifted her from that position onto his face while keeping her hands tied behind his head. He let her legs swing from his shoulders.

With his head in her crouch, he placed a vibrator in the seat of her pants with his mouth. This created an arousal from both stimulators. Just before she climaxed, he flipped her down, sat her back down in the chair, and untied her. She fanned and cursed with excitement because he had worked her up.

The next dancer came out, and everyone just stared. He stood 6'5" and was built like Michael Jai White. He came out like a beast. He was rather rough around the edges, knocking things down, and breaking them as part of his performance. Next, he pulled a

Dr. Jekyll and Mr. Hyde act. However, the ladies realized that he was supposed to be Hulk. He was more of a muscle showoff with not many tricks or moves. His tongue action took the show as he rolled it, shaped it, and let it roll out like red carpet before he kissed and licked a few of the ladies' bodies. He ended his time with fire ablaze on his tongue.

A masked performer came out last. He was dressed in a suit and tie with African music playing. He got everyone involved from clapping to standing onto their feet. His engagement with the ladies set up the performance. He chose Allie and Tabitha. He started by placing Allie's hands on Tabitha's hips and making them move to the rhythm of the music. He then joined in and switched them out just as the storytelling part of the act began.

While telling the story of a man and woman who battled wanting to have sex with another woman, the performer had gotten down to his Zulu warrior attire. He grinded, lifted, and bent Allie in ways that showed he enjoyed himself. His secret weapon was no longer a secret as the poke had come through and saluted Allie. He bowed to her and allowed her to unveil his face and find out that it was Dewayne Folkson.

The look on her face was shock, embarrassment, and disbelief. She handed him the mask and ran off with Becca and Tabitha not far behind. They rushed with questions and talked to Allie through the bathroom door. Finding out that it was Dewayne wowed the ladies, and they rushed back to him. When they got to the floor, he and the other dancers were still entertaining the ladies.

The dancers reintroduced themselves and then shared hugs and laughs with the ladies until the night ended. Before departing, Dewayne apologized to Allie for embarrassing her or making her feel some type of way. He assured her that he wanted no problems but dared not to leave without making sure she enjoyed herself. The ladies were tipsy and horny as they packed up and left. Instead of staying together that night, they went their separate ways.

Chapter 12
Tabitha

Tabitha and Dominick had been friends for months now without an official title. They had been going on dates, hanging out, taking mini-trips and sexing, but still Dominick had not met the ladies of Tabitha's life yet. Nearly every encounter included Tabitha driving… mostly with her driving to him wherever he was or going to his city. He only drove a handful of times. When he did, it was to meet her in his city or close it. Everyone was supposed to meet Dominick at Becca's wedding, which was now days away. Tabitha was preparing for his visit but refused to inform the ladies about it in case he didn't show.

While she was out with Logan and Drew, he texted and called her. To her surprise, he was already in town. The boys had not seen her with anyone else since their father two years prior. That's why when Dominick asked her to meet him, she hesitated before responding. She informed him that she had the boys and asked him to meet her at the Turkey Hut on Florence Ave. When she pulled up, he was already parked and awaiting her company.

Once she parked, Dominick approached the car wearing a ball cap, white tee, Levi jeans, and a pair of Gucci slippers. Drew and Logan were staring like detectives as they pouted and wondered who the guy was in their mother's face. With no further thought, she introduced Dominick to Logan and Drew, and the awkwardness was over. Just like that, everyone was ready to eat.

As soon as they were seated, Tabitha was approached by an unfamiliar face with an inviting voice.

"Hello Tabitha. It's nice to see you, or shall I say meet you," the stranger said.

The look on Tabitha's face was of controlled confusion as she politely responded, "Well I guess it is. Who are you?"

"I'll give you a hint," she giggled. "This point of contact is not supposed to be as nice as it has been so far, and for that you're welcome. Now to properly introducing myself, I'm Mrs. Rachel Vermont."

Tabitha's facial expression was now numb and unable to read. However, her verbal response was presented impressively vile as she stated, "What a pleasure to place such a beautiful face with a familiar name. Thank you for taking the time to walk over so that we could properly meet one another. As you can see, I'm out with my men. If you don't mind, I would like to order and finish our evening. I do appreciate you for making this encounter as nice as you did."

With an embarrassingly angry face, Rachal turned and walked off without saying another word. The looks on the guys' faces were hilarious after Tabitha's reply. It had opened the door for pettiness for the rest of dinner. Between Dominick, Drew, and Logan, Tabitha wouldn't live that moment down. They ate and laughed until their bellies were full. Dominick walked them to their car where he applied kisses to Tabitha's cheek as he closed her door and shook hands with the boys.

Tabitha dropped them off to her brother's house for the rest of weekend. When she returned home, Dominick was waiting. She parked and hurried to let him in the house. As he followed her inside, she asked that he remove his shoes. Impressed already, he obliged. Shortly after, his clothes were off as well. Her organization turned him on even more than he had already been. He'd desired her since the start of the evening.

He walked closely behind her as showed him around. He couldn't wait any longer; he had to have Tabitha immediately. So, he pushed her onto the wall and began kissing and undressing her from behind. As each article of clothing fell to the floor, he applied kisses to the newly revealed areas. Once those panties were off, he kissed her cheeks and maintained his position as he caught the flow from her sugar bowl. His tongue licked as his mouth sucked and made love to her sweetness. Each flicker of his tongue caused caramelizing sensations as she melted.

Her legs weakened after several satisfactory deposits as he ate her from behind. Flipping her towards him, he lifted her up and sat her on his face. He demanded her to verbally guide them to her room. He carried her as she fed herself to him with her legs around his neck. Never letting his mouth rest, she stuttered between releases to direct him down the hall, passing three rooms on the right and making two lefts. She warned him that he would have to take two steps down once they entered her master bedroom.

She gasped and squeezed his head between her legs as he took the first step down. After taking the second step, he slowly eased her down and guided her head to his kingdom. She kneeled to his throne as she felt the strength of his power. He stopped her after he felt the warmth of her mouth. Lifting her from below, he guided her to the bed and held her hands behind her back as if she was being arrested.

With her hands still in position, he inserted his power into her socket, and the session was lit. They gave each other electrifying performances as if they were porn stars. After reaching their climaxes, they laid alongside each other breathing hard and sweating.

Dominick laughed then smacked her on her booty. "Baby, you know what? You're my missing link."

"Your missing link?" she asked in a tone that showed that she was confused and drained.

He noticed that she was talking with her eyes closed. The dim light along her stairs illuminated her face just enough to reveal that she wasn't looking at him as he stared at her fatigued face.

"Sit up and look at me. I'm serious. You're what I'm missing in my life. You're my exclamation point. Not only do you finish my sentence, but you also give it expression."

Tabitha's position changed so rapidly that she began to tremble from nervousness.

"Dominick, what are you saying?" she asked.

Bringing himself closer to her, he snatched her back by her hair, licked from her neck to her ear, and whispered, "I want you to be more than my friend... more exclusive... be my woman. Let's take this to the next level. I want an actual relationship with you. We can make this work. You've already shown me that you care and are willing to make it work. Now it's time for me to show you that I can do the same."

Tears rolled down her face as she nodded in agreement with becoming an item with Dominick. He was everything that she imagined physically. She questioned his emotional side, but he was sexually satisfying and fun to be around. Perfection was all that she could think of at that moment. He was her missing link, too. Plus, the boys liked him. She damn near kissed his face off in excitement of their new commitment to each other. Their lovemaking session made them burn off the food from earlier. So, she jumped up, showered, tidied up, and cooked the man some breakfast.

By the time she was done cooking, he was asleep. She woke him up and walked him to the kitchen. They sat and ate French toast, grits, sausage, bacon, eggs, and fruit with orange juice to wash it all down. As they chatted over breakfast, Dominick made a confession.

"I was here for business when we met, but I found out that my homeboy lives out here somewhere. I'm supposed to meet up with him later. He's supposed to be getting locked down soon."

"Is he going to jail, or is he getting married?" Tabitha asked.

Dominick's phone rang in the room. He excused himself from the table to answer it. When he returned, he answered her question and told her that his friend had just called. He was going to shower and meet up with him. Then, he would call her when they were finished. He ate breakfast, showered, and left.

Chapter 13
The Wedding

The wedding day had finally arrived. Everyone was arriving in a timely fashion. The rehearsal had gone perfectly the night before. There was no worry besides one of the groomsmen not showing. Both sets of parents were dressed and waiting for the ceremony. Pastor Devin and Allie were the first at the church. Kami was also there, and Jackson even showed up to escort her. Dawn and Montrell had made it and brought less security than normal. Tabitha was the last to arrive and she had slipped in quietly.

No one noticed that she and Dominick had come together. Jeremiah saw Dominick come in, but he didn't put two and two together. He rushed to introduce the two before the ceremony began. They laughed, hugged, and then kissed right in front of him.

"We met months ago, but good looking out. You would have definitely been on point with this one had I not already stepped to her," Dominick said while one hand was still around Tabitha's waist as the other shook Jeremiah's hand.

"Becca said that I would like you when she told me that you wanted me to meet a friend of yours," Tabitha added before she ran to her place as a bridesmaid.

Everything was beautifully arranged. The wedding colors were champagne and gold with hints of greenery. The ladies carried dahlias and wore pearls. The elegance of the ceremony was that of a fairytale. Becca looked like a queen as her father walked her down the aisle. Jeremiah couldn't hold back his tears once he laid eyes on his bride.

As she got closer, his body began to tremble with excitement. Once Mr. Matthews shook his hand, backed up, and unveiled Becca, Jeremiah's mouth fell open. He broke down the minute he saw her without the sheer covering. Kissing her hands as he held them, he promised to love her forever. Pastor Devin wiped his eyes and began the nuptials for the two to exchange vows. The wedding was beyond words. There were no interruptions, no mistakes, and no delays. The guests blew bubbles as Jeremiah and Rebecca walked out as Mr. and Mrs. Davis.

On the way to the reception, Jeremiah told Becca about Tabitha and Dominick. She became ecstatic - even more excited than she already was. The day was surreal.

"I have always wanted to date friends with my best friend. I married you, and now I hope they work out and remain together. They make such a beautiful couple. You know how they met right?"

Jeremiah stopped her from talking by kissing her passionately. She was so happy that she kissed him the entire way to the reception. When they arrived, their guests were lined up to congratulate the newlyweds. They danced the night away, and everyone enjoyed themselves. They were all one big happy family as they laughed and took pictures all night.

Apparently, the day went too perfectly, because the drama suddenly began. Kami had too much to drink and was all over Jackson. She tried to undress him and then herself. He rejected her and she became loud, drawing attention to them. Dawn and their security guard escorted Kami to the powder room where Dawn tried to straighten her up. However, her stupidity level was through the roof.

She had threatened Jackson by stating that she would call Malik since he didn't want her. Jackson walked out on her to avoid confrontation. Meanwhile, she presented a terrible comparison of the two and made Jackson's sex game to be amateur compared to Malik's. Kami's behavior took the evening downhill. Tabitha insisted that they take Kami home. Dawn's security helped take her to the car. She ranted and raved as they drove her home where she finally passed out.

Once Dawn and Kami left, the reception continued, and everyone was hype again. The DJ earned every cent that night. There wasn't a dull moment after their departure. From soul train lines to line dancing to battles, the newlyweds and their guests wore themselves out.

By the time the Davis's made it home, all Becca had to offer was side booty. Jeremiah could not resist the feel of her vaginal suction. She knew exactly how to ensure they both were satisfied, regardless of the condition of her body. Every inch of her belonged to Jeremiah now, and she would ensure that his desires were completely fulfilled.

Chapter 14
Dawn

When Dawn and Montrell returned home from the wedding, they giggled about Kami. Dawn added that she'd never seen her on that level before. She also asked her husband to excuse Kami's actions. After laughing more regarding the incident, Montrell changed the subject to a more romantic one as he removed her shoes and rubbed her feet. Moving up her leg with kisses, he set the mood just right. Dawn had already taken off her dress and left her heels on. Her husband liked to see her in only her heels.

"Japanese Denim" by Daniel Caesar had just began to play in the background. This increased the romantic mood. Montrell sang to his wife as he took her hand to dance. By the time it got to the "ahh" part of the song, he was deep stroking into a dual release. Her legs were shaking like a tambourine.

After a brief intermission, Dawn was straddled on all fours ready for round two. She eased his dick inside her mouth as she sang the lyrics of *Love Don't Change* by Jeremih. As she blessed the tip with her vocals, she sang it back up as it hardened for pleasure. Then, she climbed on the love muscle and grinded, rolled, bounced, and finessed from the tip to the base. To fight his release, Montrell flipped Dawn onto her stomach and multi-tasked the fuck out of her. He pulled her hair, grabbed her neck, and kissed her spine without missing a stroke. He was cutting up in the scissor position and making up for all the years that they were disconnected.

The two reconnected on a different level that night. Montrell had literally stood up in the pussy that night as he stroked her from the back. Dawn had perfected the arch and took the dick from her husband however he wanted her to take it that night. It had been so long for them that she rewarded herself by having no restrictions. Since Lyric's birth, the two had not had much sex. With Montrell being gone with the team and Dawn being home with the baby, they had not shared much alone time. So, they took advantage of the moment while Pop- Pop had Lyric. With hours of pleasurable flexibility and cardio, the two redefined the Karma Sutra, engaged in countless positions throughout the upstairs and down of their residence, and then slept like babies.

Chapter 15
Ladies' Night

As months passed, everyone went on with their lives. The ladies caught up occasionally but not like they needed. It was time for them to catch up. Becca was the hostess for the upcoming ladies' night, and her new place was the location. Tabitha was the first to arrive. Her glow set the atmosphere for the evening. Becca got excited and wanted to begin the conversation prematurely before everyone else arrived. Kami and Dawn came together. The tension eased into the room upon their arrival. However, once Kami apologized to Becca, things slowly reset the mood from animosity to satisfaction. Allie showed up nearly an hour later.

This ladies' night was different from the previous ones. This time no one had intentions to stay all night. There were many distractions, since everyone's lives had changed so much. So, the ladies made a toast to life with shot glasses in the air. When it was time to throw them back, all eyes went towards Kami because she didn't drink hers.

"So, let me guess... You don't drink anymore," Becca asked, feeling disrespected. "Or, at least not since my damn wedding?"

Kami explained, "That's not it, and I just apologized to you for that. I thought we just got over that."

Without another word, she raised her shirt and displayed her pudge as she pouted like a toddler. Their faces were in shock as they looked around at each other.

"Tell me that's Jackson's baby," Allie said with uncertainty.

Kami's face frowned at her reply. "Yes, it's his. I haven't been with Malik since before he lost his wife. And, did y'all know that it's a possibility that Malik's daughter may belong to Jackson?" The ladies just stared in astonishment as she continued. "Yes! He had an entire case built around Malik and me. He had pictures, messages, receipts, and voice recordings. Malik's wife, Lauren, hired Jackson to investigate Malik. She was trying to prove that he was cheating on her.

"When Jackson found out it was me, he tracked everything down. He played the fuck out of his role, too. I had no idea how much he knew. When he finally revealed it to her, revenge was her goal. I'm good and handling everything well now. I was willing to stay since I did my dirt, and he did his. I went through a breakdown though; my life had fallen apart.

"Kaleb is with Tyson and Grace now. We have joint custody. I wasn't going to keep this baby at all. Jackson moved me out, paid everything up for six months, transferred me out his company, and took me off all his accounts. This happened right before your wedding. It's kind of why I acted out. My hormones were raging, and I was hurt. He still doesn't know about the baby. I already know he'll want proof that it's his. So, to avoid all that, I never mentioned it. I believe that's all the new info in my life."

"Bitch! You have gone through enough for all of us."

Becca took a sip and then downed the rest of her glass. Then, she downed the one that was poured for Kami.

Kami added, "Oh yeah! Tabitha, Jackson had pictures of you, too. I guess

Dr. Vermont's wife hired him, too. They looked like the same ones that she sent to your phone that time."

"Since we're mentioning that irrelevant piece of shit… Why did she come up to me when we were out eating at the turkey leg and crab place on Florence Avenue one night? I was with Dominick, Logan, and Drew so I behaved. I handled her politely, and if I tell you they had a blast making fun of me that night…" she laughed. "She had the audacity to say that I was welcome. I was supposed to be thanking her that the encounter was nicer than she promised. I should have told her to go find her husband, but like I said, I behaved myself." Tabitha explained to them.

Becca laughed. "She's fucking residents up there and staff, too. They are passing her ass around while she thinks she's fucking over Dr. V. She's only making the damn man look bad." Changing the subject, she asked, "How are you and Dominick doing? I'm so happy for you. You're glowing."

"Dominick and I are doing great. He drives here now that we are exclusive. He's the best mistake that I have ever made. He allowed me to take risks and live outside of the box that I built. Allowed me to indulge and recognize versatility I didn't know existed..." Tabitha smiled and talked about him like she was in love.

Allie added, "It's good to see you happy again, especially after so long. You're such a wonderful woman."

"You're glowing, too, ma'am. Must mean you're out of the doghouse," Dawn asked.

Allie blushed, "Devin and I are like newlyweds. We've had a fresh start. It's crazy how the birth of Champ broke us and then brought us together again. I had absolutely no doubt that Devan Dawntae Peterson belonged to Devin way before physical proof. I just lusted behind Dewayne so much that guilt ate me up. We never had sex, although I wanted to in the flesh… Anyway, you know I had the book signing. Guess who I saw there. Alfie! Topo Montego from school. I felt so guilty when I saw him. I know we're adults now, but I remember us liking one another in school, but I wouldn't talk to him because Becca was so mean and used to do him so bad."

"Bitch, I didn't know you liked Alfie. I would have eased up. He would have been brother-in-law," Becca teased.

Allie continued, "Well I told him that we should catch up - us plus Devin because I'm not trying to be back on bad terms with my husband. Do you know that he named his daughter the name that he used to call me - Anji? That's something, huh?

"On another subject, later that day after the book signing, I gave my husband oral sex in the bookstore and made love to him in the car while still in the parking lot. I wouldn't be surprised if I'm not pregnant again. Then, all our babies can grow up together. Dawn, are you trying for another one? Lyric is a good age now to stay in rhythm with baby number two. Ava and Devan's age gap caused me to be out of the swing of things. But now that I'm back, it wouldn't be bad if baby number three came."

Dawn replied, "Lyric is wonderful by herself. She's demanding more attention. But you know if it happens, it happens. Montrell wants an even number of children; he's not concerned about the sex of the child. We finally had sex after the wedding though. Being married into fame is something. It's like I don't have peace because someone is always watching. He's there but not there. It's almost worse than military spouses. He's gone a lot, but we make the best of time that he's home. Lyric knows when her daddy is home though. She smiles, kicks, tries to walk, crawls, and talks. He spends plenty time with her, and she sleeps near when it's my turn with daddy."

Allie laughed, "I bet that's how Devin felt. Well as a matter of fact, he told me that he did. Champ took all of Devin and Ava's time and attention."

Becca said, "With the amount of fucking y'all been doing, all of you might be pregnant. While I'm over here breaking in our marriage, our headboard, and my back, I'm not breaking these vows. Jeremiah is the truth. I underestimated him. I didn't think he could handle all the sides of B, but baby... He puts it down and gets it right back up. He shakes back like a pro.

"Everything has balanced out. Time with him, the twins, and for myself has been working well lately. The twins are used to everything now. I'm glad Brad is finally over his feeling betrayed season and I guess his "this is payback" syndrome. Bradley and Broderick enjoyed meeting Jeremiah's son, Noah. They're all around the same age. We have a big enough family not to add more kids."

"How was the honeymoon?" Dawn asked out the blue.

Becca eagerly answered, "It was amazing. We did just as much fucking as y'all did. Hell I might need to make sure that I'm not pregnant. Bahamas doesn't owe us anything but sleep because I promise we didn't get any. We ate, snorkeled, walked beaches, and had sex almost everywhere. We took so many pictures and videos of everything."

"That makes me think… How in the world did you afford to get Montrell and me that jet for our honeymoon?" Dawn asked.

Kami answered, "Where there's a will, there's a way. You don't need to know that. Love has no price value. And, there's no limit on the amount of favor given either."

"Well, we still thank you for that. It was a wonderful gift," Dawn said.

Tabitha's phone began to ring. It was Dominick, so she walked off to the other room to answer. After a few drinks and a little more laughter, she was ready to go. Before the night ended, Allie asked if she could pray for them individually and collectively.

She prayed, "We are too connected to be disconnected. I ask God to remove any and everything that's unlike Him. Free us from our ungodly desires and bless our lives as we choose to live for you. Cover us individually, our families, and our entirety. Father, we ask for your forgiveness for our sins that we will, have, and are committing. We're asking that the known and unknown sins and iniquities are forgiven as well. Thank you in advance for helping us to live and love right. Thank you for healing our hurts and building our brokenness. We trust you. We love you, and we thank you. Amen."

"Allie, thank you for your obedience towards your assignment," Dawn said as she wiped tears.

The night ended with tears, hugs, snot, deliverance, and forgiveness. Kami was rocking back and forth with tears falling. Becca grabbed her and whispered, "We needed this. I love you, and you're going to be okay; we all are. Trust the process."

Allie said, "I think you should come to service. We should go as a family. We always depart before Sunday and with everything that's going on, the alter can't hurt any of us more than we've already been hurting ourselves."

"That's not a bad idea at all. Fellowshipping is necessary inside and outside the church," Tabitha added.

Becca said, "We just fellowshipped at the wedding. We also come over when daddy's church is on program. We will be there though. It has been a while since I heard brother-in-law preach for real."

The ladies went their separate ways. Ladies' night had changed from a weekend to a night.

Chapter 16

Becca

After several months of marriage, Becca received her first piece of mail with Davis as her last name. It was a certified letter. As she opened it, she noticed it wasn't the form or certificate she was expecting. The first line alone crushed her spirit.

"We regret to inform you that your marriage has been denied and is invalid due to the other party, *Jeremiah Davis*, legally being wed to another body. Burden of proof has been presented to you on this day. No court date is required to annul your union. All documents have been voided. Bigamy is a crime where in most instances the other spouses are unaware of the previous one's existence. Our penal code defines the offense of bigamy in section 523:

'Whoever, having a living wife or husband, marries in any case in which such marriage is void by reason of it taking place during the life of the wife or husband, shall be penalized with imprisonment of either portrayal for a term which may range to seven years and shall be accountable fine.'

Becca was filled with anger, betrayal, and hurt. The news that she had just received in the letter literally broke her down. She fell to the floor and wept right where she had dropped the letter. For nearly an hour, she cried and prayed. Then, she gathered herself enough to contact Jeremiah. When he answered her call, his voice worked her over to a place where she had almost forgotten what she called for. Becca immediately redirected her focus towards the purpose of her call.

"Jeremiah, I just received a letter," she paused to clear her throat, "that states that our marriage isn't official because you're still married to your first wife. What I don't understand is why I knew nothing of this marriage or existence of this living wife. I also want to know why you didn't feel like you could have or should have mentioned it to me. I had to find out through a letter what you didn't have the decency to tell me. You didn't crack your fucking mouth open to tell me that you were still married or had ever been married. We've discussed so much about our pasts, but this part of your past remained a mystery. This vital information was avoided during all our long night sessions of getting to know each other. Can you tell me why, Jeremiah?"

Jeremiah had not opened his mouth to respond to anything that Becca had mentioned, and that pissed her off even more.

"Since you don't have anything to say now and didn't want to say anything about it then, don't you say a motherfucking thing later. Don't you dare attempt to explain shit to me later!" Becca snapped and hung up.

As bad as she wanted to call back and go further into the conversation, she didn't allow herself to fold. Instead, she called Allie. This was a rare communication outlet but a necessary one for the current situation. Allie answered the phone and spoke softly, hoping Becca wouldn't be her normal loud self. Surprised by Becca's tone, Allie immediately became all ears. She could tell it was a serious matter based Becca's tone and the lack of sarcasm. So, without any force or interruption, Allie allowed Becca to unfold on her own.

"Allie, I don't know what to do. Is this what God was trying to show me in my dream?"

"What's going on?" Allie asked.

Becca updated her on the dream that she had about Jeremiah, Nicole, and the wedding. Then she told her about Jeremiah already being married. Allie's position changed once she got the okay from Becca to input her opinion.

"First of all, I believe that the Lord sent your warning, but you didn't comprehend it. Secondly, that's against the law and trickery on his part. So, you should have a conversation with Jeremiah regarding the issue. Not only does this create a problem for you and Jeremiah, but it also places you at risk of a lawsuit from his current wife. If you haven't already done so, an annulment should be filed, and you should get out of that right away.

"Take care of this. Then, run and trust God for further instruction. I can't tell you what to do, but these are merely my suggestions. You were sent to me for a reason, Becca. You can take what I recommended, or you can do it your way. However, know that there are consequences worse than hurt if you put your hands on that man... even worse if you choose to use a weapon. I love you, baby sister. I wouldn't tell you anything wrong," Allie explained.

Becca was in tears at this point. "I knew it was too good to be true. There's nothing for Jeremiah and me to discuss. When I asked him, he didn't have shit to say... not a mumbling fucking word. I couldn't even hear him breathe. The letter stated that the marriage was invalid, and an annulment was already in order. I will follow up with the courts to see what to do next."

Chapter 17
Tabitha

Dominick's behavior changed within a few months of their relationship shift. He had been busier than normal and more distant than usual. It's like their relationship had drifted backwards. He hadn't been back to her city but a handful of times. She went back to doing all the driving to see him. He was allowing her to express her feelings while he avoided his. He called one night, and she could instantly tell something was wrong by the tone of his voice.

He bluntly stated, "Babe, I have to let you know this. I may have a baby on the way. She said it's mine, but honestly, I don't remember having sex with the female. She's due any day now.

I will have to get a DNA test when the baby's born. I understand if you're upset. I haven't known long, and I didn't know how to tell you. I wanted you to know just in case it's mine so that it won't fuck up what we have going."

Dominick explained his side, leaving Tabitha speechless. When thoughts were released, she went in on him.

"I found out weeks after I admitted wanting to be exclusive with you," he said.

"I should have known that things were going too good to be real. I knew it was something. That's the reason I was so hesitant to meet you. I knew that I wasn't what you were used to. You probably did randomly fuck her. That's what you do… hunt for prey and fuck on demand. Random pussy is bringing forth your child. How did she get ahold of you? Contact info? Correct, so you did more than fuck. You exchanged info and kept in touch, Nick. I'm not a fucking dummy.

"I told you from jump that I'm not who you're looking for. I'm not one of these young dumb females you prey. I have had enough games played on me. I have no time for this shit anymore. First the married guy and his shit, now you and your shit. If I was just a fuck then, you should have done that and continued with your life without fucking up mine.

"I already do too much when it comes to your ass. I don't complain about it since it was my choice, but you show no consideration about anything. You show no gentleman-like tendencies. Who lets a woman drive hours and miles alone any time of day or night to see them? I have never asked you for anything but the damn truth. I spend my own damn money. I even send your ass money knowing that you didn't fuck with me like that.

"Still, I stayed committed to you and your dick. My commitment has been to you, your needs, and your wants without knowing what the fuck you're doing or who you're fucking dealing with these bullshit lies. You probably fuck randoms left and right in my absence. Man fuck you, Dominick. I'm done," she said before hanging up.

***

Weeks later, Tabitha received a text with an attachment. When she opened it, she a picture of a newborn that came from an unfamiliar phone number but resembled a familiar face greeted her. Undeniably, the baby looked like Dominick. The eyes, nose, and lips looked like they had been cropped from his face and minimized to fit the baby's face. The next text that came through was *"Sorry"* with a sad face emoji behind it.

Just like that, there was no more Dominick. Tabitha had already blocked his number and every number that he attempted to call from before today. She also blocked the number that the picture had come from. It was good while it lasted.

Chapter 18
Kami

Kami invited the ladies over for lunch and a chat session. She had just received good news. Tabitha had already told her what happened between Dominick and her. So, Kami didn't waste any time playing matchmaker.

"Teddy is single. Have you ever thought about dating him? You know he has been wanting you for years. With him being my brother, you know I wasn't having that shit."

Tabitha hesitated before saying, "Teddy and I used to mess around before I married El Jay.

Becca heard that and said, "Bitch, you never told me that. I slept with

Teddy one day when I skipped school. Ain't that a bitch?"

Kami's face displayed shock at finding out about her brother and her friends. Dawn had just walked into the room. Kami eyeballed her before catching her off guard.

"Tell me you didn't sleep with Teddy, too."

Dawn's eyes got so big that denial was impossible.

"Can't say that I didn't. It was his baby that I lost in high school and college. I thought you knew that after all these years. That was before and after he got his pilot license, too. Oh shit. How did I forget he was a pilot? That's how you got the private jet for the wedding. That's why you didn't want to tell me."

"Don't change the subject… All three of you fucked my brother, but none of you thought to tell me. How in the fuck does that happen? Damn. I'm speechless. I don't even know how to feel about this. Here I am trying to play cupid and shit. He done shot his shot already with three of the four of you."

Kami was confused as she tried to put everything together without flipping out. Her mind wouldn't allow her to rest until she spoke to Allie. She dialed her number immediately and eased into the conversation.

"Good evening, First Lady. I'm here with the other ladies who have all revealed that Teddy shot his shot and hit bull's eye with them. So, I called to see if you were part of this history lesson, too."

Allie was floored. She was laughing so hard on the phone at her synopsis. Once she calmed down to giggles, she responded.

"No ma'am. He had sex with Becca when we were in school. It wasn't my business to tell. Teddy wasn't getting those bragging rights of having me and my sister. Now, I have to go. I'm working late. See y'all in a few if you haven't put everyone out by then."

When they hung up, everyone was looking around. Becca poured Kami another drink.

"That damn Teddy. I can't even be mad at my boy. He "gentleman'd" the fuck out of it. He kept it to himself without bashing, making us look bad, or try making himself look good. Shit I'm kind of proud of my boy. He didn't sabotage our bond. Slicker than a can of oil. And, after all these years, we've never found out until now," she said.

Tabitha looked at Becca and shook her head. Kami looked around and did the same.

"What's today?" Kami asked. "Oh yeah… Teddy is off." She grabbed her phone and dialed his number. As soon as she noticed the phone was no longer ringing, she went off.

"Korey Te'shun Robbins! Is this true about you? You've fucked three-fourths of my friends. Everybody but Allie, huh? That's only because she wouldn't give you any play since she knew you fucked Becca. Then, you knocked Dawn up. Twice?"

Dawn yelled out, "Kami! It's the past. Let it go. It's over and done with, baby. That's why we didn't tell you. You overreact."

Teddy tried to talk. "Dawn never told me she was pregnant. And, did you say twice?"

"Yes, twice… two times," Kami emphasized then looked towards Dawn in disgust. Dawn glared at her. Her fierce stare unfolded untold pain as she began to gather her things to leave. Kami stared and headed to keep Dawn from leaving while still holding the phone.

"I called you all over here to tell you the good news that happened in my life and here you go laying this on me. Thank you for coming, but like Dawn, y'all hoes can go home," Kami pointed them to the door.

Chapter 19

Becca

When Becca walked into the house, there were romantic and descriptive signs everywhere. All the notes led to a recording of Jeremiah explaining everything. Becca pressed play on the remote that was underneath a post-it that read: "Hear me out." When the video began, Jeremiah was not looking at the camera. His head was down as he began to speak. He looked into the camera with tears filled in the ducts of his eyes.

"I have been silent long enough. I don't know where to start. You know it's not like me to have nothing to say. However, you know I don't argue. I will just let you talk as I did. I was young when I got married, and it was a mistake. Like many mistakes, this came back to haunt me — only briefly. I mishandled the mistake, and it followed me. I thought that we had gotten divorced months after we were married through an annulment. I didn't think I would have to speak of it again.

"I wasn't trying to hide anything from you, B. I promise. I just knew that there was nothing that I could say that would sound believable without proof. Therefore, I had to go back home and go through boxes, drawers, and cabinets to find the documents. I was willing to go through whatever legal process that I needed to so that I could be with the woman that I love. I wanted and needed to keep you as my wife. I needed to get proof to you because I knew that words alone wouldn't make this a resting issue.

"Yes, I was married before. No, I didn't mention it to you. I'm more than sorry for never bringing up that conversation. The way that I responded, or my lack of response was juvenile, immature, and embarrassing. I didn't expect you to be okay with it, and I apologize for taking so long to get back to you. I have lost your complete trust and caused countless questions to pop up about your decision to marry me in the first place.

"That placed such a strain on fixing us. I have damn near burned my bridge that I need to cross back to you, but I have hope. I have prayed about making us right. With the proof that I'm legally divorced from her to my knowledge, some of the trust will return. I hope that you would forgive me and allow me to continue as your husband. I can prove to you that I am who you know me to be."

He blew a kiss towards the camera, and then the TV went off. Eric

Benet's *I Wanna Be Loved* played as Jeremiah walked from the back room with a brown envelope and a crown. He carried the crown on the envelope as he kneeled before Becca, hoping to crown her as his queen. He first presented the papers from the envelope. Then, he waited for her response before making any other moves.

She stared at Jeremiah after she read the letter and looked at the dates on the documents. It was dated and notarized sixteen years ago. Jeremiah explained that because his ex-wife gave him so much trouble, he made sure to get copies of his own. Becca called the court to verify, but the voicemail picked up with the message that the office was closed for the day and staff would return the following morning during business hours. Pissed again, Becca snatched the crown and threw it at Jeremiah.

She yelled, "We will try tomorrow in the morning! How could you do me this way? This is the most anyone has ever put me through emotionally. Brad had a whole bitch on the side, and it didn't bother me as much as this and we had been together since college. This shit hurts, Jay. I love you from a different place. I started believing in love again with you, and it backfired like a motherfucker. Then, after several weeks, you come home like everything would just return to normal.

"I understand that you may have thought the proof would make everything okay, but the big picture is that you didn't say a fucking word. You showed me absolutely nothing, Jay. You didn't reach out to me. You left with no fight because I told you to leave. You didn't fight to stay; you just walked away without communication. Then, boom, you want to come in here and

Boyz II Men me on bended knee with this damn crown.

"How in the fuck do you crown me if you left? What kind of king are you to abandon your kingdom? You left with no explanation. I have been open and honest with you from day one about everything. I have changed bad habits for you without being asked because I saw that there were uncomforting vibes from your end. We can work this out after confirmation tomorrow, but it won't be as easy as you think…

"I love you Jeremiah, and you know that I do. It's not even questionable how much I love you to still want us to work. We are definitely going through counseling outside of my family so there is fairness for both of us. I love you too much to start over with you. Are there anymore secrets you have hidden from me? Any more children? Are there any more women I should know about? Anyone's ass I need to beat? You know me well enough to know that I'm going out on the limb, and it's all out of love."

Chapter 20
Allie

Allie and Devin were back on good terms, the kids were growing, and life was back to normal. At least that's how it seemed until Allie noticed that Devin had not been as routine as he normally would be. He had been late picking up the children. He was behind on the bible study sessions. He was fatigued all the time, and his body language was hard to read. His mornings started early, and his nights ran late.

One night when Devin came in late, he woke Allie and asked her to pray for them. He also asked her if she trusted him. She sat up and asked him what was going on for him to ask her that. He wouldn't tell her. He just repeated the question. She told him that she did and then demanded that he tell her what was going on.

Devin grabbed her hand and begged her to understand that he could not tell her because it wasn't time. However, knowing that she trusted him allowed him to continue to move forward with the assignment. He kissed her forehead and departed from the room. Not long after, he hurriedly left the house. Allie decided that waiting to find out what Devin wasn't telling her was not an option. So, she followed him.

It was raining outside, and he was driving fast. Therefore, keeping up with him became impossible for her. Fifteen minutes into her surveillance, she aborted her spying attempt. Instead of catching up, she decided it was best to just go home. She immediately began to look for things that were out of place. Amid her search, she called Kami in hopes to receive Jackson's number. Allie was ready to build a case.

Kami was reluctant to refer her friend as another client for Jackson. Allie became overwhelmed with her thoughts and broke down during the call. Kami pleaded with her to not dig into the situation any further than Devin had given her authority to do. She suggested that she talk with him again in a few days. Kami was firm on her no. However, Allie refused to accept it as an answer. She ended the call full of frustration.

She continued to search for answers. When she found none, she finally called Jackson's office and left a voicemail. Since it was past business hours, she didn't expect a return call until morning. However, in a matter of minutes, her call was being returned personally from Jackson. He immediately began to speak.

"I got your message. I didn't listen to it all. Once I heard that it was you, I instantly called you back. Is Kami okay?" he asked with his voice full of panic.

Allie told him to calm down and that she was calling him to be a customer. He declined and explained to her that she didn't need his services. He offered to listen to her situation as she began to give him the details on Devin's actions for the last month.

"So you immediately came to the conclusion that there is someone else?" he asked.

"He's human just like the rest of us. Pastors have been known to cheat just as much as, if not more than, some of the other professions and you know that," Allie replied.

"Did you talk to Devin? Did you ask him where he has been going? I don't want to get involved in this. It's too close to home, and I don't want it to backfire. My suggestion is to talk to Devin first. Allow him to answer. If he chooses not to tell you anything, leave it in the Lord's hands and allow it to be revealed before it's too late."

"Jackson, I have to respect that. Thank you," Allie stated before hanging up.

As she pressed the end button, Devin was turning the key to enter the house. Immediately, Allie prepared herself for the talk. She met Devin at the door with a dry towel. She'd also placed a change of clothes on the countertop in the bathroom. He was drenched as if he had been standing in the rain in the same spot for a long time. As the water dripped, Allie dried him off. She began to undress him, when she noticed the shrinkage was extending to a standing position from her touch. His shiver and shake began for one reason and ended up being for another as Allie blessed the risen with sloppy head. Devin's knees began to shake from weakness as she drained fluids with her jaws of life.

Upon his release, he pulled her head in closer to absorb the fruit of his loins. She played yo-yo with it before swallowing. Devin's eyes bucked like a deer in headlights. He had never known her to do anything like that. His posture changed as his dick was at a full salute. Devin reached for Allie, politely turned her round, and inserted himself. The juices from her pussy were so welcoming. Splashes trickled all over the sofa, floor, and end table as he pounded her while holding her hair within his fist.

Their house phone had been ringing and now the answering machine light had begun to flash. This caught Devin's attention mid-stroke. To distract himself from the light, he fell back into the chair and allowed her to climb aboard. Instead of climbing onto his dick, Allie climbed onto his face and let her legs hang over the back of the chair. She grinded briefly before falling onto his dick and causing instant eruption.

When she lifted herself from his dick, he was still shooting out like a sprinkler system. He reached for her, but she didn't react the way he'd hoped that she would. She continued to walk towards the bathroom after she passed him his clothes from the counter. He got up and wrapped the towel around his waist. Then, he walked over to the table, pressed the button on the answering machine, and listened to the new messages. The last message played back first. It was Jackson.

"Sorry to decline your case, but I don't think that what you believe is going on with Devin is true at all. Hopefully, you have spoken with him regarding the concerns that you have. I also hope that you believe that my services are not needed and that you have worked out your issues. Have a great night and may the two of you be blessed. You will surely be fine. Pray about it and leave it with the Lord. Goodnight."

Devin jumped up and stormed towards Allie. To his surprise, she was pleasuring herself and close to a release when he entered the bathroom. One hand was pressed against the shower door while the other was bringing forth satisfaction that he had left incomplete. Feeling some type of way, he dared not interrupt her, especially after the way she left after his release.

Hearing her moans had him standing up again and ready to enter into her gates and suck on her pearl. At the last of her orgasm, Allie jumped when she realized Devin was in the bathroom and had witnessed her masturbation session. She noticed the rise of the serpent and invited him in while the water was still hot.

He entered the shower with his wife. Then, he kneeled and served himself from the fountain. He created a rhythm of his own that caused her to burst in his mouth as the water flowed over their bodies. He pulled her head back and lifted her against the glass. Devin slow-stroked his wife as long as he could keep his balance before she had him lying on his back in the shower while she popped, locked, and dropped it backwards on the dick.

He muscled up, keeping her booted over, and beat it up from the back. He used that moment to ask her again if she trusted him as she reached to use the wall for balance. He was fully erect and serving short thrusts with authority. Between moans, Allie answered, "Yes, Daddy!" Devin stroked faster. Allie moaned louder as her climax neared. He asked her if she was sure that she trusted him. Again, she responded in a higher pitch, "Yes, Daddy!"

Allie's body could barely handle Devin at this point. He got in five more strokes before she was shaking, moaning, and breathing hard as she reached her orgasm. He smacked her on her ass harder than normal as he rinsed her "power" off their bodies. Then, he went upstairs without another word. Before Allie could ask any questions, Devin stopped her and got right to the point.

He told her that he heard the voicemail from Jackson. He further explained that he couldn't discuss what's been going on because of the confidentiality of the situation. There would be a time and place to discuss everything, but the time had not come yet. He kissed her forehead and then turned over and laid down to go to sleep. She was left speechless and irritated.

Chapter 21
Tabitha

"To prevent you from losing your license, I left that facility. I have avoided you at all costs. I have chosen to move on to show you that there is nothing between us. You're married, and I'm not looking for trouble from you or your wife. I have enough going on without the drama that you're trying to cause. Whatever infatuation you claim to have, I need you to get ahold of it before someone gets hurt. Now, make this the last time that we have this conversation," Tabitha said to Dr. Vermont.

Just as she was hanging up from Trenton, Dominick was pulling up. Before he could knock, Tabitha snatched the door opened and her hands went straight to her hips. She stood waiting for him to explain his reasoning for popping up to her house with no form of notice. She was already upset from the conversation that she'd just had with Trenton, so there was no sympathy for Dominick. He informed her that had driven up to introduce her to his son. She flipped out with no filter.

"How dare you think that this shit was a good idea! You're bringing a baby that you had with another bitch to my front door looking pitiful. You and your baby can take your asses back where you came from."

As angry as Tabitha was at Dominick, the way she felt about him was real. She played hard, but she still had a soft spot for him. Forgiving him seemed so much easier with him being right there in front of her. She figured that the baby had to have been conceived prior to their relationship because he was not quite three months. He was so adorable. Maybe Dominick was being honest.

These thoughts and others crossed Tabitha's mind as she contemplated accepting him and his baby whose name was Nicholas. They'd come so far from where they'd started to just end the way they did. She loved him too much not accept the part of life that he was in right now. She opened the door and allowed them to enter. Finally, she listened to his side of the story without interruption.

As soon as he finished talking, he asked her if she felt comfortable enough to hold Baby Nick briefly until he stepped to the restroom. When she held the baby, she felt something uncomfortable in his clothing. To her surprise, there was a tag still on the baby's clothes that hadn't been snatched off yet. She walked to her kitchen

drawer and used scissors to cut it off.
When they walked back into the den
area, Dominick was sitting on the couch
with a blank look on his face. He was
looking at a ring that he held in his
hands. Tabitha paused and asked if he
was okay. Dominick looked up at her.
Then, he took the ring out of the box
and kneeled to propose. She grabbed his
hand and assisted him up.

"I don't want you to do that. Don't
ask me to marry you. Right now my
answer will be no. I want to try with
you and see where we go."

He looked into her eyes, kissed
her on the forehead and said, "I never
said that we had to rush into marriage. I
just know that you're who I want to
marry and spend the rest of my life
with. I told you that you were my
missing piece... my exclamation point.
You bring me joy and make my life
make sense. Will you wear my ring,

accept my proposal, and let's move forward? I promise not to bring drama to your life. Furthermore, I promise to be the man that you need and want. I promise to bring you the simple things that you long for, see you when you feel down, kiss your scars, embrace your moments, be your other half, and love you for you."

With a straight face, Tabitha looked at Dominick while still holding Nicholas.

"What about him? I can accept him, but I won't accept drama that may come with him, now or later. You told me that his mom left him with you with no intent to return since he was a mistake and so were you. But what happens when she wants him or you? What happens when he's no longer a baby and she decides that she wants to be that mommy to get her baby back after we establish love and a happy home? Did you think about that?"

Dominick dropped his head and tucked away the ring. Then, he immediately took it back out and placed it upon her finger.

"We will be just fine. The five of us will be a happy family. She made the decision to walk out, and I took the legal steps to make sure that I'm in the clear as we move forward with our lives. Do you think that I wouldn't consider the possibilities before buying this ring to make you my wife? I know what I want, and I know who I want. I want you to be my wife because there isn't another woman that I'd rather spend my life with.

"I've told you multiple times that you complete me. The completion is necessary for me. I need you. I want you, and I need you. You make me feel like the lyrics of Eric Bellinger's 'Day

After Forever.' Every girl in my past was a waste of time. I want us to be together… from now until the day after forever…" Dominick sang with tears in his eyes. "I want to tell your father that I'm in love with his daughter… You're my queen, and I want to be your king until the day after forever."

He kissed her hand and pleaded his love for her in hopes that she would understand its depth.

Chapter 22
The Unexpected

The phone rung at 2:43 a.m. It was Becca calling Devin.

"It's time to tell her," she said before hanging up. Devin tapped Allie's shoulder after he had already gotten up dressed the kids. He rushed her to get up, get dressed, and get to the car because there was an emergency. She jumped up and hurried downstairs to the car. As they drove, Allie sent questions flying out left and right. Devin finally explained to her what was happening.

"You remember I kept telling you that it wasn't the time to tell you. Well, now is the time to let you know that your mother has been sick. She didn't want you to know so we had to keep it to ourselves. She wasn't willing to fight with you about her decisions to let the sickness run its course while she handled the consequences accordingly.

"Well, the course is coming to an end, and it's time to find out the results. I have not been cheating on you. There has been only one other woman - your mother. I have been doing my part in taking care of her and making sure that she doesn't look like all of the dealings that she has undergone. She has been a beast in handling it all, too.

"I'm really surprised that you didn't know or catch on. Even after you told me about the dream that you had and the conversation that you had with God; I couldn't say anything. I know that it's a lot to take in so suddenly. But the way you deal with things and with all that you had going on, I didn't want you to neglect any of your assignments."

Allie cried and prayed all the way to the hospital. When they arrived, everyone was already there - Becca with Jeremiah, Tabitha with Dominick, Kami with Jackson, and Dawn with Montrell. They had the waiting room full. The nursing staff had asked them to wait until there was updated information about Mama Matthews. They sat and waited as one big family. The children were there half asleep while the adults gathered with inquiries and concern. Allie approached Becca and slapped her.

"You're my sister! How could you not tell me about Mama? After I listened to your breakdown about this woman's husband, you couldn't tell me that our mother is sick. And you, Kami," she said as she directed her focus to her friend. "I got the two of you into counseling so you and Jackson could bring this baby into the world together, especially knowing that there is no way Lauren's baby could be his. Tabitha, you could at least have mentioned that something was wrong instead of just focusing on your rejection of Dominick's proposal but accepting the role of stepmom to his new baby. And Dawn, I won't even get started with you because I know that you knew."

Pastor Matthews stopped her and passed her an envelope that had "Allie-Cat" written on the front. Allie opened it and began to read it aloud.

"As I go through the aches and pain of this stage of cancer, no one knows because I keep it to myself. I'm not in the mood for pity nor sorrow. As I sit here writing this, the pain in the left side of my body is excruciating and powerful. However, I don't want it to get the best of me. I don't want it to place me in a situation where I'm no longer able to do for myself. Right now, I see myself as self-sufficient and strong-willed. I

don't want life to take the wind from my sail.

"Each day I have been grateful that He saw fit to awaken me from the slumber in which I was placed the night before. That shows that I still possess favor over my life. I thank God for my immediate family. I thank God for Frank and my girls. I know that this is going to hurt Allie Cat more than Becca because she's the one who tries to help and save everyone. I don't want her to save me, so I have been keeping this from my darling angel. Becca is my strength; my powerhouse. She will probably get the blame, but she's only doing what I asked. If you're reading this now, things have gotten to the point where I don't have much time.

Just know that I'm at peace, and I have done right by God's word."

Becca hugged Allie as she dropped the letter to the ground. Pastor Matthews wrapped his arms around them both as the doctor came in with the face of disappointment. Without a word, everyone broke down.

The doctor looked at Pastor Matthews. "She doesn't have long. She asked for Allison only."

Allie quickly followed the doctor to the room where her mother laid. Not much verbal conversation was held between them while holding hands.

Allie repeatedly asked, "Why Mama? Why wouldn't you let me be there with you through this? Why did I have to be the last to know?"

Mama Matthews gripped Allie's hands tighter as she tried to explain with her restless voice. "Allie Cat, you have been a wonderful daughter your entire life. I knew that you wouldn't want to let me go. I know that you have so much going on, and I want you to enjoy your success."

She turned her head to receive a kiss from Allie. Allie kissed her jaw. Just as she raised up, she saw that everyone was standing at the door and easing into the room. The family enjoyed the last moments of Mama Evelyn Matthews with laughter, tears, and music until she took her last breath.

Pastor Matthews read a few scriptures as he was the last to let go of his wife. Slowly everyone left the room and returned to the family waiting area. They engaged in small chatter until Pastor Matthews interrupted.

"Wait a minute... Everyone has been reaching out to Allie about everything, and I know now is not the time to discuss it. But I know that Mama would have dug in deeply to revive the love in this room. I know that we all need to get our lives together right here and right now. Becca, did you and Jeremiah get your marriage reconciled? Kami and Jackson, have you made the decision to stay together? Tabitha, you accepted Dominick's proposal. Do you plan to marry him? Dawn, have you had the discussion with Montrell? Do you know that communication is the key to marriage? Allie, do you forgive us for fulfilling your mother's wishes?"

Before anyone could answer, Brad walked in with the twins and his family. Becca's face was filled with disrespect as she hurried towards him. Jeremiah grabbed her arm and reminded her that Brad is no longer worth the scene that he knew she was on her way to create.

He whispered to her, "Don't start, B."

She snatched away and Pastor Matthews interjected, "Thank you for coming, Brad, and for bringing the boys. I wanted all the family here."

Becca added, "Now y'all can leave. I will let you know what the arrangements are once they're finalized. You can pay your respect then."

Then, she walked back over to Jeremiah. He embraced her, and she placed her face in his chest and screamed when she heard the elevator close behind Brad and his family. Jeremiah held her tighter.

"How dare he bring that bitch up here upon Mama's death. She could have easily stayed in the damn car. She's petty as fuck for that. He is, too. Just disrespectful!" Becca whined loudly.

Jeremiah walked her off to the side and talked to her calmly. He was trying not to upset her too much in the moment that she was having.

"Babe, you were just as disrespectful to me. I was trying to stop you from making a scene and embarrassing yourself and the family. You snatched away from me and carried on as if I was invisible. The two of you had history being married for so long and all. I understand your anger, but just like you need me here, he needs her by his side. The boys didn't need you acting out either.

"Mama Evelyn means a lot to everyone here. Pops called him to make sure the boys were here. He hopped up and brought them up here immediately. Come on, babe. Forgiveness is in order. The both of you have moved on and appear to be happier apart. You should be mature enough to be cordial to each other past the hurt and betrayal. I love you, and I would much rather correct you in private as your husband than in public. Counseling has taught us too much and brought us too far to go backwards."

Becca accepted every word that Jeremiah spoke to her. She apologized to him, and they walked back around to the family room. Everyone said their goodbyes. As they were headed out,

Allie stopped and openly forgave everyone.

She explained, "I forgive you all for your roles in Mama's wishes of not telling me. I also forgive you for your opinions of me and the way I handle things. I want to thank each of you for trusting me though. If you didn't you, wouldn't have had me distracted during the process of Mama's condition. She knew what she was doing and so did God. He showed me this exact moment, and I just didn't understand it when I saw it.

"Before we depart, let me say this… It's all going to work out for each of us. We are not perfect. There will be messes and turmoil to come into each of our lives, relationships, and minds, but it's our job to continue the process. Devin, let me first thank you for choosing me to be your rib. Thank you for seeing me for who I am. Your dedication to our marriage and our family shows so much about you. Thank you for staying beside me this entire ride.

"Jackson, thank you for using your advice for my marriage to revive your marriage to my sister. This baby is not what saved your marriage; God's reality check did. Montrell, your rekindling with Dawn brought forth new life and happiness. That's just what she needed. God sent you at the exact time, and He kept her around after a reality check. Once she saw that you would be there after that attempt, she knew it was real between the two of you. He showed her better than anyone could ever told her, so thank you.

"Jeremiah, I was iffy about you after I found out about your past. I told my sister to run away and don't look back. I also told her not to kill you... I'm laughing but so serious. Thankfully, she listened to God and not me. All legal documents were presented, and all skeletons are out the closet. I noticed how you just handled the situation with her this morning. Thank you. Lastly, Dominick, you brave man. Risking it all for the woman that you love… I know she hasn't given you the answer you want yet. Now is the time to ask her again…"

Tabitha looked at Allie with threatful eyes that also contained fear and excitement. Dominick passed Nicholas to Becca and kneeled before Tabitha again. He began to sing the words to Eric Bellinger's song again repeatedly.

"Every girl in my past was a waste of time. I want us to be together…from now until the day after forever… Every girl in my past was a waste of time. I want us to be together…from now until the day after forever…"

She smiled and nodded her head. He asked if she would marry him, and she finally agreed to his proposal. After placing the ring on Tabitha's finger for the second time, he rose up and asked if Pastor Matthews would marry them. With no hesitation, the pastor agreed. Then, he quickly declined and asked if Devin would do the honors. Devin gladly accepted. As everyone cheered for the happy moment in their time of sorrow, Pastor Matthews walked back to the doorway where Mama Matthews last laid.

He fell to his knees. Everyone rushed to him as he cried a cry that no one had ever heard before. No one had ever seen him at a loss. Suddenly, he grabbed his arm and nurses rushed over to him. After a quick visual assessment, they rushed him back to a room as a patient. Becca knew exactly what was going on.

She looked at Allie and asked her, "Do you remember when we were kids, and I woke up from that dream of Mom and Dad walking and holding hands? I never saw their faces, but I knew it was them because of their love. Well, this is the moment. Daddy is holding Ma's hand again. I feel it. I saw it as he walked to the doorway."

Just as she got the last word out, the doctors came out the door with the same look that they had hours before.

"Mr. Matthews suffered a heart attack and didn't survive it," one of the doctors bluntly informed the family.

They looked around at each other in shock. Allie and Becca just held each other. They wept but seemed to be at peace knowing that they'd just lost both parents yet realizing it was love that brought them together. That same love that they had for each other allowed them to depart hours apart.

Allie stated, "I think it's beautiful how Dad's heart couldn't survive without Mom. In just a few hours, look how fast life happened. Dad made sure that we made peace in his presence. Mom made sure that she left peacefully and that we were all here together."

Becca added, "They were all about living right and bonding. This shit hurts though. Dad made sure to teach us what to do in times like this. Crazy thing is that he knew. He said what he had to say, did what he had to do, and was loved for it all. Damn, now we have to plan two funerals and lay both parents to rest while remaining sane and trying to be strong."

No one left until everything at the hospital was done. Afterwards, they all met at the Matthews house where they found wills, insurance policies, and specific burial instructions laid out on the table. There was also a note that read:

"Girls, we love you and know that we raised you right. You always made us proud to be your parents. Don't let it stop because we transitioned, and don't let us have to discipline you from where we now reside. 🙂

If you're reading this letter, that must mean that our time has come to an end on this Earth. Therefore, you have found that everything was laid out to make this time a little easier on you. It's not going to be easy, but we tried to make it simpler to organize such a big loss for you. You have everything you need. Everything is already paid for and arranged for the most part. You will have to take this to the funeral home and ask for Steph. She knows exactly what to do from there.

We've set up a private ceremony for us just for you all. A memorial service will be held at the church, which I left for Devin and Allie to continue our legacy if they wish. Hopefully, they will accept it. We are leaving the house to Becca and Jeremiah. Everything else has been notarized and is included within the information on the table. We love you both. Equally."

Chapter 23
Final Chapter

The day of the ceremony arrived. Both Pastor and First Lady Matthews laid beautifully before immediate family and friends. The service was short and sweet, and everyone remained strong until the bodies were rolled out to the final drive. They were placed in a vault and stored at a mausoleum close to where they lived. They rested side by side in the indoor burial option that they chose. That's where both Allie and Becca broke down. The love of the family was shown effortlessly as everyone supported them.

After the service, everyone met back up at the Matthews' house where Devin married Tabitha and Dominick in a private ceremony. Before the ceremony began, Devin had to go into the home office of Pastor Matthews where he found an envelope with his name on it. It contained five sets of rings and a note that read:

"Devin, I need you to be overseer of the couple's ministry that starts with the five of you. Rededicate your marriages. Make sure Tabi allows Nick to marry her because it's been appointed by God. I may not be exact with the sizes, but I'm close. I have enclosed a disc. Just insert it and follow the directions. Everything will work itself out."

Devin did just as the letter instructed. All marriages were renewed, including the brand-new marriage between Dominick and Tabitha. There were arrangements for girls' nights, guys' nights, family nights, and couples' nights. The couples toasted, ate, and mended bonds. Their friendships remained with losses and gains. Most importantly, their bonds became stronger with insight and acceptance.